Reincarnation

Reincarnation

SUZANNE WEYN

SCHOLASTIC PRESS/New York

Library of Congress Cataloging-in-Publication Data

Weyn, Suzanne.
Reincarnation / Suzanne Weyn. — 1st ed.   p. cm.
Summary: When a young couple dies in prehistoric times, their
love — and link to various green stones — endures through the ages
as they are reborn into new bodies and somehow find a way to connect.
ISBN-13: 978-0-545-01323-9 (hardcover : alk. paper)
ISBN-10: 0-545-01323-2 (hardcover : alk. paper)
[1. Reincarnation — Fiction. 2. Time and space — Fiction.
3. Love—Fiction.] I. Title.

PZ7.W539Re 2008   [Fic] — dc22   2007008743

10 9 8 7 6 5 4 3 2 1   08 09 10 11 12 13/0

Printed in U.S.A.   23
First edition, January 2008

The text type was set in Augereau, Dalliance, and Syntax.
Book design by Leyah Jensen

For David Levithan.

Thank you, thank you (thank you) for yet again
taking a chance on me and always "getting" what
I'm trying to say. It means so much.

Special thanks to Diana Gonzalez, Colleen Salcius, and

David M. Young for reading as I wrote and giving me their

valuable comments; to Pam Laskin, Bill Gonzalez,

Rae Gonzalez, and Nancy Krulik for their interest and

encouragement; and to Karen Weise for letting me research

emeralds in her great home library.

SW

Reincarnation

Start

And the next thing I knew

I was a baby.

So I begin.

We begin . . .

Prehistory

The flickering campfire played across the full belly, wide hips, and torso of the faceless figure chiseled into the cave wall. May stood beside her fire, staring up at the goddess, mesmerized by the vision.

The shadows moving over the uneven rock surface made the engraving's left hand appear to caress her swollen midsection. Her raised right hand shook the crescent-shaped bison horn she clutched. For a fleeting moment, the formerly featureless head flashed with a face of unspeakable beauty and power.

May wondered if this was truly a trick of light and shadow. Or was it a delirium produced by sleeplessness or the trapped smoke of the fire?

No one knew any longer who had chiseled this image of The Great Mother into the cave wall. Yona, May's mother, said it had been in the cave since the time long, long ago, when the thundering slabs of frigid whiteness first began to thaw and allowed The Growing World to return.

This conversation had come on the first night of her monthly blood. All the clan's young females spent it alone with The Great Mother. It was also the night of Yona's big news: "After the glowing sky creature devours itself thirteen times, and thirteen bloods have passed, you will be ready to leave my fire and join Lenar as his mate."

"Lenar has asked for me?" May had inquired eagerly. Yona nodded, causing May to shiver with delighted excitement. Lenar was strong and pleasant to look at. The other young males followed his lead. As Lenar's mate, May would be highly ranked among the females. A high ranking meant a place in the cave closer to the big fire, a chance to partake of the kill right after the males had finished, and all the best of clan life. May welcomed the chance to attain this status. As the female child of a female without a mate — Yona's mate had died hunting — May would only acquire status if she was well mated.

From that time onward, May had watched Lenar with acute interest, trying to hide her glances, though not always succeeding. She could tell when he was aware of her eyes upon him from the way he pulled his broad shoulders back and swiped his thick brown hair away from his forehead. He postured for her benefit, she knew.

Lenar seldom spoke to her, for it was not customary for the young males to spend time with young females. Yet May saw enough of him to slowly become disturbed by what she observed. He repeatedly mocked and struck a young male who seemed to have stayed a child though his body grew as the others did. Once, she saw him kick the hare that old blind Asa kept as a pet, just because it had crossed his path as he was passing by.

Gradually, painfully, her delight at being the one selected by Lenar faded. She wished it had not, for she desperately wanted the privilege he offered. Still, the idea of being mated to him did not fill her with joy.

But when she told her mother of her misgivings regarding Lenar, Yona insisted that nothing could be done. Her unbreakable pledge had been given.

Besides that, Lenar was the best match May could ever hope for. The Great Mother would curse Yona and May both if May rejected such good fortune, which surely had come from The Great Mother herself. Angering Her was something to be avoided at all costs. If they enraged this powerful force on whom all their lives depended, who knew what disaster She might bring down upon them in Her fury? Even worse, She might abandon them, plunging the world back into The Time of Ice. Did May want to risk that?

May stopped questioning and gave herself over to the ecstasy of the vision she was now seeing of The Great Mother on the cave wall. It had been sent to her. Done with doubt, she lifted her arms to The Great Mother. The moment had come to ask for what she needed.

"Would you curse me, Mother, if I did not become the mate of Lenar?" she asked. "They say you would, but I do not think that is so."

This wondrous mother who cared for the whole of The Growing World surely saw how wrong it was for her to be mated with Lenar. Surely May hadn't been born to spend her life serving such a self-swollen, boastful mate, cringing at his touch.

"Mother, how do I escape this? Show me a sign that will tell me what to do!" May hung her head miserably. "I swear that I will serve you all the days of my life if you free me from this fate."

The smoky air stung her eyes and she shut them. Moments later, when she gazed up at the sacred engraving again, The Great Mother stood as She had been, faceless and unmoving. Her hand had returned to its resting place on Her large belly. The etched bison horn in Her upraised hand was still.

Had the magic passed, the holy moment been lost, with no response to her plea?

Maybe not: May stepped closer to better see the spark of crystal green stone embedded in the rock. It was flecked with gold and shone. And it sat directly in the center of The Great Mother's belly!

It gleamed with the colors of The Growing World, rich with the many greens, both the deep and the light, of the grasses and leaves, the mosses and ever-changing riverbeds.

It was the sign.

The Great Mother was answering her.

But what was She saying?

Kye squatted on a flat stone outcropping above the gorge. The warming sun felt good on his broad, sloping brow. It made him linger a bit longer before returning home with his catch of three hares, which he had bundled together with vine.

Many feet below, the white, crashing water raced along in a thunderous torrent of foam and spray. Nearby, an insect's trill was high and steady. What interested him most was the chattering birds coming from the forest behind him with their pattern of call and response. They were talking to one another as surely as The New Ones spoke to one another.

It seemed to him that he was encountering The New Ones more than he ever had before. When he was younger, his group hardly ever crossed paths with theirs. The exclusive territories of the two clans were unofficially defined but mutually understood. Or at least they had been. More and more, there was conflict when The Ancient People and The New Ones endeavored to fish the same section of the river or hunt the same herd of bison.

The Ancient People would surely be run off their territory by these New Ones if they did not find a way to possess The New One skill of meaningful sounds.

These things were in Kye's thoughts as he left the rock and lumbered home, the meager results of his afternoon's hunting in his hands. On the steep rock path leading to the cluster of three caves where his people lived and worked, he met his mother. Across her shoulder, draped to her waist, she wore a rabbit-fur sling crammed full with the tall, bendable grasses she used to sew fur skins and weave basketry. Reaching out, she thumped her son on the back affectionately. He grunted good-naturedly and rubbed her hand in reply.

When Kye and his mother arrived home, the area outside the three caves was alive with unusual activity. Kye was glad that the meagerness of his contribution to the night's meal would be overlooked in the excitement.

His younger brother, Ato, punched his arm excitedly and gestured for Kye to follow him into the main cave. There he waved his arms under the drawings of the thundering bison that roamed the valley. This was the time that every male in the clan anticipated with enthusiastic exhilaration. The number of the giant beasts they could bring down now would determine if they lived abundantly in the time to come or would have to survive on reindeer and hare until the next migration.

Kye's mother joined her sons. Looking at Kye meaningfully, she placed her hand on the cave drawing, and he knew what she was telling him. In the next light they would hunt and the males would have their eyes on Kye. It was his first bison hunt. If he hoped to be leader someday, as was his right as son of the leader, it was crucial that he hunt well.

With the first dawn, May emerged from the cave. Blinking against the gray morning light, she stepped onto the rock ledge that jutted out just wide enough to allow passage around to the side path that led back into the forest. At its edge, the cliff plummeted nearly a mile before it reached a racing, white-foam gorge at the bottom. Beside it, a forest thick with towering trees let out to a wide, open valley of rolling fields.

Something scurried from the cave. May smiled down at the gray weasel that had been drawn to her fire. He'd brought her a tiny dead rodent as a gift, and May had let him stay.

Now the weasel curled up a short distance away as May gazed out at the land stretching before her. Sure-footed, she was unafraid of falling from her elevated perch and went out to its very edge. Fog rolled through, obscuring the treetops and the curving hills beyond. The glowing sky torch rose higher into the sky, sucking the earthbound cloud up with it. Faintly, the rumble of rushing water reached her from the distant gorge. Gazing into the open fields beyond the forest, she realized something was moving down below — dark shapes, and many of them.

May realized what she was seeing: These were the huge beasts whose immense, furry carcasses provided so much to her people. Every cycle, they passed through at this time of the season. Having been away these last two nights, she had missed the preparation and had nearly forgotten.

Much smaller figures soon emerged from the forest. Hunters. Lenar would be among them. It would be his first bison hunt since passing his initiation rites. She tried to pick him out from among the figures, but it was impossible;

he was too far away. They advanced on the bison, fanning out along the edges of the herd.

From May's high vantage point, she spied something the hunters could not yet see. Other figures ran out into the field from the forest some distance away. This group might be more Clan People hunters coming in from a different direction, though this would have been unusual — the hunters usually stayed close to one another. But if they were *not* of The Clan People, were they from the other clan, the frightening Ice Beings who had roamed the world since The Time of Ice?

Crouching, May leaned forward. The two groups moved toward the animals on diagonal paths that would soon intersect. They did not see one another for a long while — and then suddenly, they became aware of one another's presence. It was clear from the way the two groups suddenly ran toward one another.

The Ice Beings and The Clan People had both hunted the mighty creatures for many cycles, living far enough apart that the beasts passed through their different hunting grounds at different times. Lately, though, the numbers of Clan People had increased. They had moved into larger and larger caves ever closer to The Ice Beings. There had been many skirmishes, though none as big as the one May was now witnessing.

As she watched the battle below, a hopeful thought came to her. Instantly ashamed, she snuffed it out before its tiny spark could light into flame. She'd thought it, though; there could be no denying that.

Perhaps Lenar would be killed in the fight.

Maybe this was the gift, the release from living death that The Great Mother meant to bestow on her. If so, May would be ashamed to have caused his death. Still . . .

. . . it would make her life much better.

Kye opened his eyes and slowly turned his head, taking in the nearby field visible through the forest. The sky torch was low, throwing long shadows. He lay at the base of a tree, his arms and legs outstretched. Pushing up slowly on his elbows, he remembered being wounded in the fight and fleeing into the trees before collapsing here.

Pain banged in his head, traveling like a line of fire along the sides of his skull into his jaw. When he touched the spot where it ached, he winced sharply and pulled his hand back, alarmed at the hot liquid he'd felt. His palm dripped red. He wiped it on his chest.

Where were the others? Even the thundering beasts were gone.

It was not the way of The Ancient People to simply leave a fallen companion behind.

Perhaps they could not find him.

Staggering to his feet, he leaned heavily against the tree. Had he been dead and come back to life?

He had not seen spirits of his ancestors. They had not

come out to guide him to The Great Bird who would carry him to the spirit world.

This was what he'd been led to expect in death. It was what the old ones sought when they went on their dream walks, preparing to depart for the spirit world.

For Kye, there had been only blackness — and now he was back.

He forced himself to move forward. This part of the forest was unfamiliar and the day's light was dying. All he knew for certain was that he should travel in a direction away from the sinking sky torch. If he didn't find his way before that one guide was gone, he'd be deeply lost.

Memories of the battle cascaded a torrent of images into his mind.

He'd locked eyes with The New Ones hunter just as he had raised his spear. The lean, flint-eyed male had towered over Kye, his muscular arm raised, white-knuckled hand gripping his spear.

Kye had lowered his head and charged in the way of the butting mountain ram. If he knocked this foe off his feet, he could easily overpower him. But at the moment he made contact, The New One thrust his spear down hard. Kye bolted to the right as the spear cut him across the forehead.

The New One thrust his spear again, this time jabbing Kye in the throat. Gasping for breath, and with blood from his forehead blinding him, Kye stumbled away. Another jab would finish him.

He ran for the cover of the forest.

Remembering how he had fled made him flush with shame.

Had he disgraced himself? Would The Ancient People think his cowardly actions made him unworthy to be their next leader? Would they be right?

Perhaps it would be better if he didn't return home at all, if he let them continue to believe that he had been killed fighting The New Ones.

He trudged along with no clear direction. In the dying light the forest was alive with the movement and sound of darting creatures and rustling leaves. Wings echoed overhead and Kye was not sure if they were birds or bats.

He was not going to make it out of this forest before dark, not with his mind cloudy from the head injury he'd suffered. The movement of animals in the undergrowth made him mindful of finding some kind of shelter for the night.

He walked a bit farther until he came back to the gorge where he'd lingered the day before. He spied a natural rock bridge seeming to lead into the vertical face of a rock cliff. Looking up, he saw that it ascended very far up but that there seemed to be a cave above its ledge.

On the other side of the bridge, a narrow path ran along the base of the cliff and turned inward, entering the mountain. Perhaps a more gradual ascent lay within the rock in the way that melting ice often carved paths and caves within stone. Maybe it would bring him to the cave above.

A night spent in a good cave would let him heal and give him time to consider what he should do next. He'd have to be cautious and make sure the cave was uninhabited, which meant hiding and watching for a long while. If it was empty, he would spend the night there.

Lenar stood in the entryway of the central cave, arms folded, nodding agreeably to the passing well-wishers who offered him their praise for his part in the successful hunt. He watched as they crowded excitedly around the massive, horned beast that he and the other Clan hunters had brought down once they had defeated The Ice Beings on the hunting field. Though it had been a group effort, Lenar had been the one to first plunge his spear deeply into the bison's side, dropping it to the ground.

The admiring people held torches against the darkening sky. In the eerie jumping light of the moving fires, the immense creature threw a huge wavering shadow as though its spirit were hovering protectively outside its carcass.

Word was spreading through The Clan of how fiercely he'd fought against The Ice Beings. Even when one of their squat, hairy hunters had charged him, barreling into his stomach with his misshapen, bony head, Lenar had managed to wound the savage and chase him from the field. He'd killed two others by the time the whole pack of them retreated into the forest.

In truth, he had been startled by the ferocity and vigor

of these Ice Beings. The wild fury in the eyes of The Ice Being as he raced toward him, growling and with his thick, muscular arms outstretched, had truly terrified him. He was able to bring his spear down on his attacker's head in time, before the powerful beast-man could rip him apart with his massive hands. It made him proud that he'd thought quickly enough to survive the attack.

Gaj, their leader, was approaching, the edge of his reindeer-skin cloak trailing in the dirt. He had already donned the heavy elk horn necklace that he wore for the traditional celebration after the kill.

Gaj put his hand on Lenar's shoulder, a signal that the younger male was permitted to raise his head: a sign of approval. He spoke words of praise to Lenar, and Lenar responded with humble thanks. Gaj's mate had birthed only female children. Gaj was watching the males carefully in order to select his successor.

He kept his hand on Lenar's shoulder as he steered him over to their great prized bison. Lenar's eyes traveled among the cheering crowd, searching for May. He'd pinned his hopes on this moment. He had been counting on this day going well as a way to impress her.

Though May was not of high rank because her mother's mate was dead, no other female intrigued him in the same way. He recalled clearly the day he first noticed how lovely she had become and realized that he longed to touch her. But her beauty wasn't the only thing. There was power in her. It shone from her eyes and could be read in the sureness of her movements. It was in her to be the mate of a leader, his mate.

He recalled the disdainful way she had gazed at him when he kicked old blind Asa's pet hare from his path. A hare was food — it had no place running freely among them, leaving its droppings to foul their eating quarters. If blind Asa wanted it as a pet, it was the responsibility of his mate to clean up after it and keep it penned. By kicking the animal, he'd shown that he knew and respected the ways of The Clan, and that he would not let softness for one keep him from doing whatever was needed to maintain the good of the greater number. It was a gesture Gaj would have witnessed with appreciation, even if May did not.

If May saw him now, so revered by the people, she might understand where he was headed, why he behaved as he did. She would see all the good things that she would partake of as his mate, all that he had won for them.

Sha, another female of The Clan, smiled at him; her eyes lit with admiration. He knew Sha would gladly have him as a mate. She had her own allure, with her bright eyes and reddish-brown curls, but she was not May. She did not possess May's beauty or her sureness. It was only May that he wanted.

Where was she?

Gaj pulled an axe from the belt of the fur tunic he wore

beneath his cloak. With a powerful swing of his arm, he brought it down on the creature's head, severing one of its impressive curved horns. The beast's hot blood spurted and it ran down Gaj's arm as he presented the horn to Lenar.

"You will lead after I am no longer," Gaj announced in the language of The Clan.

Bowing his head deeply, Lenar accepted the honor, thrusting the horn into the air for all to witness. All around him, the people thundered their approval, shouting and pounding on the beast, shaking their torches excitedly so that sparks flew through the darkness. The scene swirled around him under a fat, yellow, night-sky creature that stayed especially low, as though even *it* had come unusually close in order to see Lenar's triumph.

Looking up, he stared into the cheering, moonstruck crowd, willing May to appear, if only by the sheer force of his desire to see her there — and to have her see him.

She was not there. And it caused a frustrated rage to roar within him.

May knew she was expected to return. It was dark once again and she was long overdue.

Somehow she could not bring herself to leave the peace of this solitary perch. Was Lenar still alive after the battle and the hunt?

He had probably survived. He was fierce.

But as long as she did not know for sure whether he was dead or alive, there was hope. She preferred the not knowing to the prospect of returning to discover the truth.

A snap in the bushes made her turn sharply toward the sound. The weasel was awakened from its curled sleep and lifted its head.

She was being watched! The feeling was strong.

Standing, she peered into the darkness. Whatever had made the sound was in the brush by the path, near the side of the cave. Not moving, hardly breathing, she waited.

A breeze lifted a handful of dead brown leaves that had collected at the cave's base. They lifted and fell, rustling along the rocky ground.

May relaxed her shoulders, inhaling slowly. *Anything* could have made the sound. As her anxious pulse quieted again, she settled back on the ledge, watching the glowing night creature continue to climb the light-speckled sky. The night creature was especially full and round, glowing yellow in the darkness, a color different from its usual silver light.

May felt The Great Mother's presence all around her — in the breezes ruffling the leaves and trees, in the chirp and buzz of night insects. She heard it all as a song.

She began to hum, her voice plaintive, aching to reach The Great Mother, the longing so intense that it became physical. Making musical sound released the loneliness, fear, and confusion. The sound suffused her body, pouring from her mouth, lighting fires of feeling within her. This new emotion made her chant higher, wilder, until her voice was an aching throb lifting into the night air.

Though her song was all ache and wail, she prayed to The Great Mother as she sang, using the language of her people. "What use is a green stone? Reveal your meaning, O Mother! Is it a treasure I can use to be free of Lenar? Will it give me rank of my own?"

She continued to sing as her mind raced.

A rank of my own.

That must be it! With the green rock, she would gain rank without Lenar. She would be the keeper of The Clan's treasure.

There were female spirit women who had rank due to the healing secrets of plants they possessed and knew how to use. The stone that The Great Mother had shown to her would give that kind of rank to her, as well.

But where else could this valuable green rock be found? She could not dig it out of The Great Mother's belly.

Her song grew higher, louder, and more desperate. She stopped making words and let her song become pure musical tone. This desperate chanting welled up from the base of her being, filling her with emotion.

Feeling safely hidden by a bush, Kye listened, captivated by the female's song. When she had arisen, alerted by the branch he'd snapped, he'd considered overtaking her. She would be a prize he could bring home to make his people forget his shame in the battle. He might even keep her for a mate.

That idea pleased him, for he felt drawn to the female. She raised a keen desire within him.

He got onto his haunches, considering if he was truly strong enough to win a scuffle with her. Blood had stopped running from his wound and was caking on his face. His head throbbed but he was growing used to it. Yes, coming home with this female and claiming her as his mate would help his situation.

She walked to the ledge overlooking the valley, and sounds such as Kye had never heard before poured out of her mouth. It reminded him of the drumming his people loved so well, but it was higher and flowed magically around her like rushing water. She was making the talk of The New Ones. But to whom was she talking?

There was sorrow in her heart. Her sounds infused him with that same pain. He became suddenly, overwhelmingly sad.

Her form was still lovely but, to him, it had also become radiant with her suffering, the grace of her lifted arms, the desire written across her face.

His desire was now tempered with another feeling. He had connected to her in a way that was mysterious, even frightening. All he could do was listen, rapt with awe as she sang in the night's light.

He cursed his softness.

What kind of male *was* he? He had run from the battle and now he was so touched by a female's plaintive wail that he would not — could not — take her by force!

A breeze sent dead leaves running away from the base of the cave. The weasel had awakened and pounced on a mouse that had been slumbering beneath the leaves. Kye's eye was drawn to the movement, but he soon forgot about the mouse struggling in the weasel's jaws.

Something more captivating had been uncovered when the leaves blew away.

In the moonlight, a brilliant green light sparkled at the base of the cave.

He'd seen green rocks like these before, usually embedded in coarse stone. Sometimes there were flecks of it in cave walls. It was rare to see an entire stone this large all in one piece.

This was the prize he would bring back instead of the female!

His people would value it even more highly than a captive. He would say he had fought a New One for it. It would restore his prestige, his pride. And he could spare the female.

He decided to wait until she departed or slept, and then he could chisel the precious green stone loose.

Slowly turning, the female spied the green rock just moments after Kye saw it.

Her song trailed off into the air as her face lit joyfully. Kye had never imagined anything as lovely as the rapturous smile she directed at the stone.

Digging in a hare-skin bundle, she produced a flint-blade knife with a bone handle. Deftly wielding the knife, she eagerly hacked at the surrounding black rock that held the treasure fast in its grasp.

Kye leaned forward, watching avidly. He couldn't let her take the green rock. He had to get it from her. Now!

Slowly, he rose from the bush. She was so intent on her work that she didn't see or hear his approach. He paused a moment at the side of the cave, looking down on her feverish activity.

He longed to explain his situation to her, to request that she give him the prized rock and let him depart with it. He did not want to fight her for fear of causing her pain. Even more, he didn't want to be at odds with this lovely creature.

He took a step closer.

The female's head snapped back. Wide-eyed with fear, her every muscle tensed as she held tight to the knife stuck in the rock.

"Mine! Go!" she barked fiercely, waving him off. "Go!"

He did not know her words but he understood. He shook his head and thumped his chest, taking a step closer.

Her eyes grew wider. A shiver shook her shoulders for the quickest moment.

"Mine!" She shrieked in a voice he could barely recognize as the exquisite thing he had just heard. This voice was all rage, aggression, and desperation. It was a voice he could deal with.

Boldly approaching, he knocked her aside with one powerful sweep of his arm. Her knife slid across the rocky ground and he seized it. He used it to come down on the rock once, twice. Three shattering blows was all it took for him to dislodge the gemstone.

Moonlight played on its indents and turns. Peering into its depths was like gazing into fathomless water hardened into rock. Surely the power of the green growing earth was captured in its brilliant hardness. His people would be right to hold this treasure in great awe. He would be their hero for bringing it to them.

The green prize suddenly flew from his hand. The female was on his back, pounding his wounded head, screaming with the wild fury of an injured animal.

The pain made him furious, and he hurled her to the ground with greater force than he had intended.

The stone lay on the ground. He bent to seize it.

The female ran into him, leading with her shoulder.

He staggered backward, though he kept hold of the stone. He recovered in time to see her charge toward him again, her enraged stare locked on the stone in his hand.

She slammed into him more forcefully, throwing her entire weight onto his arm.

This time he was seriously off-balance, and she was locked onto his shoulder. Instinctively, he reached for something to hold on to as he felt himself lose balance.

The back of her neck was the first thing he found to grip.

She screamed in his ear, her voice no longer combative or aggressive. She was screaming in terror.

At first he did not realize how tightly he was gripping both her neck in his one hand and the stone with his other. His only thought was to hold on — to keep from being knocked down.

Nor did he understand, until seconds after that, that they had stumbled backward off the high cliff. There was nothing beneath their feet now and they were turning, spinning.

Still he held on to her, unwilling to release his grip. He would not let go of her or the green prize.

They were plummeting, locked together, toward the gorge below.

Then

I hear the sickening sound before we even hit the gorge. A bone has snapped. It rings up into my ears, vibrating in my skull.

There is no pain.

The Ice Being tumbles into the racing water beside me, his eyes wide with terror.

Then there is another Ice Being. His face is softer. He looks at me and I gaze back at him.

For a second.

A surge of water pulls one Ice Being away, the one with the stunned wide-open stare frozen on his face. The other Ice Being begins to rise toward the surface of the water.

I swim after him, wanting to know where he is going.

Breaking the water's surface, the insistent call of an overhead bird makes me look up to investigate. I have never seen a bird this large; not even the great gliding birds of prey have such a wingspan. Slowly, its great wings spread, and it spirals toward the water.

With darting eyes, I search out The Ice Being and find

that he still is in the gorge, but is now surrounded by other Ice Beings. They are not of this world. I know this because they hover just above the water. The Ice Being begins to rise into the air and they touch him, aiding his ascent, lifting toward the sky along with him. Together, they sail up to meet the descending giant bird. They let go of The Ice Being male as the bird grips him in its talons. I watch the bird fly away with him as the others fade.

I realize that I must get out of this icy water. I am already so late getting home. They will all want to hear how I fought The Ice Being and survived. They will gather round tonight by the fire and I will tell them.

The current is strong: I will have to swim like the water beasts if I am to free myself.

A thing from the depths of the river rises behind me and I turn quickly to see what it is: a face, pale and crazed with terror. Dark hair tangles around it; the head is bent at an angle that is painful to see. Shoulders, torso, belly follow. An arm springs up, fingers splayed, jostled by the current.

It is me! I am staring in horror at myself.

But I am here at the same time.

I slowly understand that I have split apart from my broken body — and yet I still exist.

I cannot make sense of this.

I am here. I exist. Then what is this twisted other floating in the water beside me?

The broken self is caught in a wave and sinks again just below the river's surface. Racing water carries it downstream, around a jutting rock, and then out of sight.

I begin to understand what has happened to me.

I scan the sky, searching for a bird to carry me away.

No bird comes for me. No spirit ancestors.

What am I to do?

And then I begin to rise above the river.

I sail through the blue sky and pass into a black, light-sparked night.

My mouth opens. The back of my head falls away. Stars shoot through me.

The top of my head floats off painlessly.

That part of me that is me at its center gives way. I am scattered, dispersed among the stars.

I am blissfully blown apart. Terrified by the shattering, yet so willing to go.

Swirling balls of fire soar through light-spattered darkness and I watch them, awestruck but not afraid.

I watch them for a long time.

Voices speak to me in whispers. They ask me questions. I don't know the answers.

I do not know why or when it is that I begin to float in a certain direction. I am on a river, traveling the current.

I come to what I think is a waterfall. I see that it's not water — but light. White light standing tall as the oldest, most giant of trees, inside a crystal pool.

As I swim into the pool, my thoughts grow so vivid that I can't tell if I am voicing them or not. I have the sense that it all has to be expressed before I am swirled into the vortex of the towering light.

Great Mother, do not abandon me.

Show me your sign again. Return your blessing to me.

Where is The Ice Being who took it from me?

Make him return the prize he stole.

I want rank of my own.

Do not let me freeze in another time of ice.

Do not make me mate with a male I despise.

I am floating in a warm darkness. Time has returned. I am aware of the moments passing in every beat of the steady thunder that pounds everywhere around me.

And then, once again, the river begins to rush. Again I am carried forward.

(On the Wheel of Rebirth)

Tetisheri, my baby girl. We name you for the queen of old now entombed at Luxor. May our divine mother, the goddess Isis, bless you. Let her son, Horus, the falcon god, always watch over you. We are not rich, but your father is respected for his craft. May you grow in beauty and talent so that a wealthy, powerful man may take you as a wife.

Egypt, 1280 B.C.E.

The sun blistered Taharaq's back as he pulled on the oars. The bitterness in his heart was not lightened by the increasingly lush beauty of the palms on either side of the rushing Nile, nor the silver crane that spread its majestic wings as it flew from a marshy inlet or even the comical hippo that rose to observe the passing barge before submerging once again.

All these sights only meant that they were nearer to Luxor and farther away from his beloved home in Nubia, the home that he might never see again.

The young Egyptian officer at the bow of the long, narrow boat snapped a whip over the heads of the laboring prisoners. The striped headpiece he wore shielded his head and neck from the burning sun. The golden cobra at its center flared brilliantly, its glare occasionally blinding. A golden cord around his neck boasted a single gleaming medallion in the shape of a golden fly, an Egyptian award for military valor. His white linen tunic, knotted firmly around his trim waist, gave him a look of cool authority over his laboring, sweating, black-skinned prisoners.

Sweat coursed down Taharaq's sides.

The officer snapped his whip once more. Had it hit,

Taharaq didn't know whether he would have been able to contain his rage. These men, his fellow prisoners, were proud men, archers so skilled that their prowess was legendary.

Taharaq glowered at the whip-wielding officer, filled with hatred. More than any other of the guards, this arrogant captain raised a murderous fury within him. When this Egyptian even glanced his way, Taharaq felt the stinging humiliation of defeat more keenly than at any other time. Perhaps it was the captain's smug self-assurance; whatever the reason, Taharaq had never known another who evoked these feelings in him.

As though suddenly aware of the electric surge of Taharaq's loathing, the Egyptian officer's head snapped around and he stared directly at him, his harsh expression full of warning. Taharaq lifted his chin, intending to meet this man's challenge with proud defiance.

But the moment their eyes locked, Taharaq was once again slammed with shame. A wave of nausea hit him like a body blow and he looked down at the moving river, frothing at the side of the boat. He knew such a movement gave the appearance of subservience, and he detested himself for it.

When he looked up again, the Egyptian captain stood beside him. "You and I know each other, don't we?" he snapped in his native Egyptian. "Where did we fight?"

Taharaq understood his words since Nubians had traded with their neighbors in Egypt for many centuries. Most

Nubians were familiar with Egyptian culture, including the language.

Yes, Taharaq thought. *It makes sense. He must have been the one who hurled the spear that wounded me. Why else would I detest him so?*

He was sure he had seen those flinty eyes before. He remembered them clearly — they had been filled with contempt, just as they were now. He felt that the Egyptian had to be correct — they had fought each other.

And yet . . . it was impossible.

He was an archer but had elected not to join the other archers on the shielded roof of a high building. Instead he'd stayed on the ground, firing from behind a tree. They'd thought he was brave, taking the first line of defense. They didn't know his terrible secret.

He was terrified of high places, always certain he would fall to his death.

It shamed him but there was no overcoming it. It was a terrible, overwhelming fear that he'd had since babyhood.

When it became clear that they were losing the battle, the other archers began to flee from the rooftop. Noticing activity on the roof, he'd looked up to see what was happening. That was when a spear had hit him at the base of his throat. When he awoke, he was in a pen with other soldiers. There was a bandage over his wound and he slowly discovered that he could no longer speak.

"Answer me!" the Egyptian barked.

Taharaq could only shake his head.

The Egyptian raised his arm angrily to strike.

"He cannot answer," the young Nubian behind him interjected urgently in Egyptian. It was Taharaq's brother Aken. "He was hit in the throat."

Taharaq winced, squinting into the sun. His right temple throbbed with the sudden onset of the fierce, searing headaches he'd suffered ever since he was a child. He'd been given every sort of potion and herb, to no avail.

His mother had taken him to a priestess who pushed away the black curls at his forehead, revealing a straight, reddish-purple birthmark. "This is the cause," she'd said, tapping her finger on the birthmark. "I know not the cure, but the gods of The Other World are telling me this is the cause of the boy's pain."

Tetisheri checked her image in the highly polished brass plate hanging on the wall. With the tip of her hennaed red fingernail, she smoothed a smudge in the black kohl liner rimming her brown eyes and plumped her shining black hair. She had lived through fifteen full cycles of the night sky and in the last several cycles she had learned all the beauty secrets of womanhood. She hoped they would all work in her favor in the next moments; so much depended on everything going well now.

She made eye contact with the harpist who played out in the courtyard. With a nearly imperceptible nod, the harpist indicated that Tetisheri should come forward.

Gliding gracefully out, Tetisheri struck a pose.

The rays of Amun-Ra, the sun god, shot brilliantly through her crisply pleated, white linen tunic, highlighting the transparency of the fine cloth, marking it as top quality. It wouldn't hurt that the sun god's fire would outline her figure to good effect as well.

The golden band wrapped around her straight, thick, black hair grew warm against her forehead.

She smiled coyly at her audience. Across from her, the nobleman Nakht, his wife, Renenutet, and their exquisitely dressed guests sat at tables by an inlaid pool with white lotus flowers floating languidly on its shimmering crystal waters. They were merchants, politicians, and dignitaries. One of the guests was an immensely fat woman who had a pet alligator on a leash. Tetisheri hoped she'd fed it well before arriving.

She waited for the harpist to hit a particular, pre-arranged note before breaking her statue-like pose and beginning her song. It was a popular tune that recounted how the goddess Isis frantically searched for her murdered husband, the god Osiris, in the afterworld, never losing faith in their love for each other, even in death.

The song challenged her vocal ability with its ever-mounting intensity, requiring her to strain to the top of her range, but it would show off her voice well. It was important that Nakht be made proud in front of his guests, so it would be clear he could afford to employ a top-quality singer and dancer in his household. Her job depended on it.

Living in her small room in Nakht's lavish estate with its murals, golden mosaics, and imported glass windows was so much more than she could have hoped for as a wife down in the village. Up until this chance arose, being a wife had been the only future she could look forward to, and it had always struck her as a living death of dullness. But since the day Renenutet had heard her singing in her father's shop and asked to hire her as the household entertainer, her life had changed dramatically. This life was more than she had ever dreamed of.

A sidelong glance revealed that her audience was watching with rapt interest. Good. This evening was crucial. If the guests responded well to her, Nakht and Renenutet would give her a permanent position in the household.

She continued with the song of Isis and Osiris, reaching out dramatically, warbling with the anguish she imagined Isis must have felt when she was told that the god Set had murdered Osiris.

Pulling back her shoulders, her arms raised, Tetisheri strained for the song's often elusive high note. Her voice quivered, cracking slightly. She pushed harder for the note. The shakiness left her. She hadn't failed entirely. As she majestically lowered her arms, she thought she saw appreciative nods.

Tetisheri began swaying her hips. The miniature bells on her ankle bracelets jingled when she kicked her right foot forward and hopped backward onto her left. Raising her arms into the air again, she hoped the thick golden cobra bracelet wrapped around her upper arm would flash with dramatic effect.

As she turned in a circle, re-enacting Isis becoming a falcon in order to better search for her beloved, she felt the animal-sense tingle of a gaze upon her. Cutting her eyes to the doorway, she glanced toward the young man standing there.

His striped headpiece with its highly polished golden cobra shaded his face but she recognized him just the same. She had grown up with Ramose in the town, but she hadn't seen him for some time. He had grown strikingly handsome since the last time they had spoken, and she'd heard he'd been made a Captain of the Guard in the army. The golden fly that hung from his neck was a mark of valor in battle.

Nakht stood and raised his hand to the harpist to stop playing. Tetisheri stopped as well, stepping back beside the harpist, her head bowed.

Nakht beckoned for Ramose to approach, and he stepped forward. "Ramses the Second thanks Nakht for supporting his successful campaign to suppress the Nubian rebellion and for raising funds for the building of the great temple at Abu Simpel," Ramose said in a formal, official tone. "In gratitude, he sends you this Nubian slave captured in recent battle."

Another Egyptian soldier dragged out a man with skin the color of blackest ebony. A wide, blood-spattered, white bandage crossed his throat. His hands were bound with cord and his legs were shackled, but still his eyes blazed defiantly.

Tetisheri stared at the man, horrified — and began to shriek, screaming in blind terror.

He had come to kill her.

She was sure of it.

Trembling, she clutched the harp, toppling it, as she crashed to the courtyard floor.

Nerfi, the household servant assigned to tend to Tetisheri, mopped the singer's sweaty brow as she lay on her sleeping pallet, unconscious but breathing heavily.

She'd be all right. Nerfi crossed the room and studied herself in the polished metal plate on the wall. With a quick tug, she adjusted the straight, bright red wig she wore over her shaved head. It was cooler and more attractive than her own hair, which she'd have liked to be black and straight but was, instead, a dull red with curls that bent at odd angles. The wig was highly preferable. She liked the bright redness, anyway. It made her stand out.

Above them was a mural of Isis protecting her baby son Horus from the rival god Set by hiding him in the reeds of the Nile. Nerfi's eyes wandered up to the mural and she sighed. No wonder people were treacherous and untrustworthy.

Even the gods quarreled, murdered one another, and plotted revenge. How could people be any different?

But what had this Nubian slave ever done to Tetisheri to warrant such a reaction? How was it possible that she even knew him? Nerfi had been pouring beer from a large jug when the commotion began. She hadn't even noticed the Nubian until Tetisheri screamed.

Now the young woman stirred and then bolted up to a sitting position, searching the room wildly. "Where is he? Is he gone?"

"They took him away," Nerfi assured her. "Why are you so scared? Haven't you ever seen a Nubian before? There are a lot of them in the police force these days. They come north for a better life up here in Luxor."

"It's not that he's Nubian. It's him, himself." Closing her eyes, Tetisheri shuddered. "He terrifies me."

Renenutet entered the room and stared sternly at Tetisheri. "Good. You're awake. My husband is displeased with that display. You have upset him greatly. He wants you to leave at once."

"She thought that slave was a spirit, come up from the world of dead beings, sent by Anubis the dog-headed god himself," Nerfi rushed to her defense, improvising the best story she could think of. "Anyone would be frightened."

Tetisheri opened her mouth to protest but Nerfi pinched her hand and she shut it again, taking the hint.

"This is no reason to be troubled," Renenutet told Tetisheri, obviously believing Nerfi's excuse. "The Book of the Dead clearly tells us that the underworld is a place where our lives are judged and evaluated so that we may begin again in another life. That is why our tombs are so well prepared, so that we can have the things we need for the perilous journey to our next life. Tetisheri, you need not fear the underworld."

"But it's still frightening. It's a life in *another* world, isn't it?" Nerfi insisted.

"If you are found worthy you will go directly to the next world. If not, you may have to return to this one to acquire further enlightenment."

"You come back from the dead?" Nerfi inquired, puzzled by this.

"You are born again as a baby into a new body. Most of the time you are born into the body of a family member. That is why babies sometimes look like a grandmother or grandfather or a deceased uncle or aunt," Renenutet explained confidently.

"I'd better get enlightened here and now because I don't want to be some messy baby again. I'm done with that!" Nerfi laughed.

A servant came into the room and spoke to Renenutet in low tones. At his words, the woman gasped, tears springing to her eyes. Quickly, she dashed from the room along with the servant.

"I'd better go find out what's happened," Nerfi said, hurrying behind them.

When she was alone, Tetisheri sat on the bed looking up at the mural of Isis and her son, the falcon god Horus. Of all the gods and goddesses, Tetisheri had always loved Isis the most. Even as a child she'd loved to gaze at pictures of her on walls and pillars, sure that the beautiful goddess cared about her, that she had a special place in her great heart for Tetisheri. Somehow she was sure Isis would understand how she felt. She was a mother, after all. She would take pity on Tetisheri.

Closing her eyes, she spoke quietly. "Mother Isis, help me, for I am so scared. I am sure the Nubian slave means me harm." These words made her voice catch. "He will kill me. I know he will."

It made no sense, yet she knew — was absolutely certain — that he would take her life. And she didn't care what Renenutet thought or what anyone else thought — she did not want to go to another world or another life. She wanted this life and no other. "Does that make me evil, Isis? Is it wrong to love the life you have — to cling to it?"

Stretching out on her pallet, she shut her eyes. Although she had not intended to sleep, she drifted into a dream. The Nubian slave was with her on a ledge, high up. His hand clutched her roughly behind her neck. Suddenly a green sphere appeared in a black sky, spinning between them. He abruptly let go of her, reaching out for the sphere. She reached, too.

They both wanted the green sphere so badly. They stretched until they could go no farther, and then went farther.

She slipped from the cliff. He grabbed her arm. Together they tumbled down into a tunnel — a bottomless, never-ending tunnel. . . .

She was shaken awake by Nerfi. "Hurry! Nakht demands to speak to you right away."

Taharaq sat huddled in the small room into which they'd thrown him. He was humiliated by the way that singer had become convulsed in terror at the mere sight of him. Was his black skin so horrifying to her? Egypt was full of Nubians. Was this young woman from some country outland so far to the north that she'd never seen one of his people?

He pressed his clenched fist against the throbbing spot on his forehead. The shards of intense light breaking in through the slatted window splintered before his eyes. The only thing that would make this curse abate was sleep. He knew it from the countless times before, so he leaned his head against the cool clay wall and let dream-filled slumber carry away his pain.

He was outside. The palm trees were gone. Strange plants he had never seen before whispered below him. From the cliff he could see their tops swaying. It was a world of tremendous green everywhere.

His hand clutched something coarse and thick. He was trying to steady himself but his bare foot continued to slide beneath him.

There was a girl with him. Her coarse hair was what he held. It was Nakht's singer, though her sleek hair was now unruly and knotted. Her eyes were wide in terror.

She was screaming.

He wanted to comfort her. "I won't hurt you." But he did not have the words.

He did not have the words!

So he clutched her more tightly.

Suddenly a green sphere appeared in a black sky, spinning between them. The sphere would save them!

Its magic was the answer.

He reached for it, not meaning to let her go. But he stretched too far.

She slipped from his grasp, tumbling away.

It took a moment to realize that he, too, was falling, hurtling down a tunnel that seemed to have no end. . . .

He awoke with a start. The singer sat across the room, staring at him intensely.

Why had he dreamed of her?

Why was she in front of him now?

"Ramose is on guard outside," she warned, standing. "If I scream, he will kill you. He has promised me that."

The slave scowled at Tetisheri but said nothing. "Could you speak before you were injured?" she asked.

He nodded almost imperceptibly.

They gazed at each other, expressionless. He was oddly familiar to her — but that was, no doubt, because he had been in her strange dream.

Her reaction to him was still powerful, but she forced herself not to let it overwhelm her. There was too much at stake for her now. She would be brave, like Isis.

"Nakht has told me he is displeased with my reaction to you," she told him. "I do not want to be sent home. I have prayed to Isis and she has taken the terror from my heart. I hope you will not hold it against me in the future."

He did not nod or consent. Did he even speak Egyptian? Many Nubians did, but she could not be sure. It seemed, though, that his expression softened a bit. He had stopped glowering at her, at least.

"This day, the mistress of the house has learned that her father has died," she went on. "They are already preparing his mummy. My father is a pottery maker in the next town over. Nakht is sending Nerfi with me to buy four canopic jars from him. You are to go with us to carry our supplies. Ramose will accompany us. I have been told that since he is from my village, he is being sent along as a reward for his service. But, I suspect, he has been sent to report back to Nakht on whether you and I can get along."

Tetisheri heard coldness in her voice that she had not intended. Rather than have her voice shake and betray her fear, she held it steady through great effort. Nonetheless, she could tell that the resulting tone was not warm.

He continued to stare at her steadily, his face revealing no emotion.

"We will keep our cordial distance from each other and make the journey together. All will be well in that case," she concluded, heading for the door.

As he had promised, Ramose stood guard outside. "All went well?" he checked.

"He just sat there," she confirmed.

"Do not fear him," Ramose assured her. "He is afraid of me. I will be there to protect you."

"I dreamed of him," she confided. "He knocked me off a high place."

"Dreams are but phantasms of the mind," Ramose said. "You were frightened by him and your mind concocted a fearsome tale. That is all."

"I have heard our spirits travel in our dreams," she said.

He grunted dismissively. "It will be good to go home. They are right to buy their canopic jars from your father. His workmanship is the finest."

Tetisheri had always loved the jars when she was young. Four jars each with a different lid, representing the four sons of Horus: Hapy the baboon, Qebehsenuef the falcon god, Duamutef the jackal, and Imsety the human. Then she had discovered their purpose. Each held a different organ taken from a mummified body — the lungs, the intestines, the stomach, and the liver. They were entombed along with the owner's mummy. From then on she could never separate the jars from their function, and lost her love of their fanciful lids.

Her father often chided her for her distaste of everything to do with death. "It's a change much like the shifting sands of the desert," he tried to convince her. "Your *ka*, your spirit double, will roam after death. It may want to return for things it needed in this life. That's why we must supply them."

But she would have nothing to do with it. She loved this earth, the sun on her face, the call of birds, the smells of oils and burning lamps. She was too much of this world to ever want to leave it.

"My father *is* the best potter," she agreed, shaking off the thoughts of death.

Ramose stepped closer to her. "I will enjoy spending time with you back in our village as we did when we were children."

She was suddenly uncomfortable and turned to leave, but he held on to her wrist.

"Back then we liked each other, didn't we?" he said.

She knew he meant more than mere childish liking. It was true. There had always been something unspoken between them. "But you went away and joined the army," she reminded him.

"Strange," he said, "back then I always had the feeling that *you* would go away and never return, leaving me to wonder what had happened to you. It was such a strong belief, yet it was based on nothing."

"So *you* left instead?" she guessed.

"Yes. I left you before you could leave me. But I am grown now and no longer believe in such foolish premonitions. And now we have found each other again."

She studied his face. It was handsome and strong. What was it that had bothered her about him before? She couldn't remember. Had she thought he was too harsh, too cold? None of that was apparent now.

As a girl, she had been almost relieved when he'd left for the army, but now he was back and he interested her all over again.

Tetisheri held his eyes a few minutes more before sliding her wrist from his grip. "We will get to know each other again on our journey, and perhaps the past will reawaken," she said.

The sun burned down on Nerfi's shoulders as the group made its way through the desert sand on the trip back to Nakht's manor. The ebony skin of the slave beside her glistened with sweat as he strained to pull the sled laden with their supplies. In her large basket, she carried the four canopic jars they had purchased from Tetisheri's father. They would be home before Amun-Ra left the sky.

Just ahead, Tetisheri and Ramose walked along, talking together. Nerfi lifted a heavy jug of water from the slave's sled and hurried ahead with it. "I have brought water for you," she offered Ramose.

Ramose undid the flask tied to his sword belt and Nerfi poured water into it. Then she turned toward Tetisheri and stumbled. The heavy jug filled with water crashed onto Tetisheri's foot. It cracked in half, making a puddle in the sand. Screaming with pain, Tetisheri teetered back a moment before collapsing onto the ground.

Nerfi threw herself onto the sand beside Tetisheri. "It is the heat," she cried. "I am overcome from it. Do not punish me."

Ramose scowled at her. "Get up, fool. You deserve to be whipped for such carelessness."

"Leave her," Tetisheri admonished. "I need your help."

Ramose bandaged Tetisheri's foot, which grew swollen almost instantly. He tied it up with linen from his army supply bag. Then he pushed aside supplies on the sled and made her a bed, commanding the slave to pull her the rest of the way home.

Tetisheri's added weight slowed him down and he soon fell yards behind Ramose and Nerfi. The sun was growing lower in the sky. "We do not want to be stranded out here after dark," Nerfi said to Ramose. "Perhaps we should hurry ahead to send back servants to assist the slave."

"She's right," Tetisheri agreed when the cart had caught up to them. "Leave the slave behind with me. We will be all right until you return, and it will impress Nakht that we have stayed behind together without incident."

Ramose unsheathed his sword and brought it to the slave's face. "Do not even look at her," he barked. "If I hear that you have done anything to worry her, I will gut you and throw your insides on the desert sand for the jackals to devour. No one will care. Keep pulling this sled. Do not rest for even a moment."

The sled jutted forward and then stopped. Tetisheri turned onto her side and strained to see what had happened. The slave's hands were bleeding, and the blood ran down the rope. He was on his knees, clutching his head.

How far ahead had Ramose and Nerfi traveled? They were specks in the distance. Good. This slave did not need Ramose's fury laid upon his shoulders. How much pain could a human being endure?

Her past fear of the slave deserted her as she limped around to the front of the sled. In this condition, he posed little threat. "You are ill?" she asked.

He pressed his hand onto his forehead, his eyes clamped shut. She took some linen from the bag Ramose had left behind and wet it, then pressed it to his forehead. Her hands working quickly, she untied him from the sled. When he was free, he began to draw the Egyptian hieroglyph for sleep in the sand.

Nothing but sleep would staunch the agony of his pounding head.

Tetisheri recognized the symbol. "Yes, sleep if you must," she agreed. "Go back on the sled. Sleep." Staggering to the back, he curled into a ball and slept.

Tetisheri sat in the sand, her back supported by the bundles on the sled. Amun-Ra was preparing to depart, spinning orange and low in the sky, taking the worst of the extreme heat toward the ground in his descent.

When she tried to rotate her ankle, pain shot through her like a stabbing knife. It was more than physical agony that caused tears to jump to her eyes: How would she dance with a broken foot? Nakht and Renenutet would surely send her home now.

The trip back to her village had been disorienting. Ramose had returned as a hero. Tetisheri had been greeted as a sort of royal figure as well. Everyone assumed she would wed Ramose, even her parents, who were clearly delighted at the prospect. Somehow it seemed inevitable.

A mewing sound came from the covered basket sitting among the bundles at her back. Stretching around, she took it down and reached inside to check on the small black-and-orange wild kitten she had found during the visit home.

The villagers enticed the feral cats with scraps of food so they would come to their yards to eat the rodents that decimated their grain stores. This little one had been wandering in her parents' courtyard with no mother in sight.

Renenutet kept statues of Bast, the cat goddess with the feline head and the body of a woman, all over the house. Bast was a daughter of Osiris and Isis, the twin sister of Horus. She was the keeper of his sacred Eye. She was also the mother of the lion god, Mihos. Surely Renenutet was a lover of cats and wouldn't object if Tetisheri brought this pet into the household.

Tetisheri reached into the basket to check on her new pet. The kitten clawed playfully at her hand, nipping her. "You're a frisky baby," she said. "Settle down. We'll be home soon." Taking it onto her lap, she stroked its soft fur until it purred.

In little more than fifteen minutes, the slave was up again. He bowed and began to tie himself to the sled. "Is your head better?" she asked as she returned the kitten to its basket.

Touching his forehead, he nodded. His eyes were bright, refreshed. She stopped and looked at his dark, desert-lined face and saw him as if for the first time. His face was not her idea of classic beauty, not like Ramose with his almond eyes and long, straight nose, but she saw something there that drew her.

"Sit with me a moment more," she entreated him.

As he settled tentatively beside her, she drew in the sand the hieroglyph for peace.

It was unusual for anyone other than a priest, priestess, or royalty to be able to read or write, but she had learned a little from her father while working in his shop. They sometimes had to inscribe an urn, jar, vase, or canopic jar.

He nodded his agreement and responded with two hieroglyphs: *No harm.*

She smiled a little and he answered with an equally slight smile.

How she wished he could speak. She wanted desperately to talk to him right then because she now felt the need to patch together the links that connected the information she already had. He was a captured soldier. He could write in Egyptian hieroglyphs. He had some illness that pained his head. And she had dreamed of him, dreamed of him so deeply that it was as if she had drunk in his spirit.

Was this the *ka* of which her father had spoken? Had their *ka* spirits met in the dreamtime, each clutching for the mysterious green jewel? Was that why the feeling of knowing him was now so strong?

Was it why she had feared him at first sight?

Was the fear warranted, an omen?

Were they destined to tumble down some endless tunnel together? In a flash, she saw the image again in her mind's eye. A shudder of fear ran up her spine and made her shoulders quiver.

On impulse, she drew two stick figures in the sand. She depicted them tumbling from a cliff. She pointed to herself and to him.

He stared at her, his face filled with amazement. Then he nodded vigorously.

She drew the sign for sleep and gazed up at him with an inquiring expression.

Yes! Yes! He nodded and began to draw. He put together the pictures that made the sounds for *dream*.

He knew!

They *had* met in the dreamtime. She was sure of it now. He had experienced it, too.

He drew a circle between the two stick figures she'd drawn. "Amun-Ra?" she questioned, knowing it was the sign for the sun.

Shaking his head, he began to write in the hieratic script educated people used when not writing in formal hieroglyphics. She was able to read it, again because her father had taught her to write basic bills of sale.

He wrote: *The green orb*.

She nodded excitedly. "Yes! We both wanted the green, spinning jewel!"

Thrilled with their growing realization, they had drawn close to each other, their noses nearly touching.

But now they drew away from each other warily.

Something about the green orb had frightened them both.

Tetisheri didn't know where to look. She could no longer meet his eyes.

He also looked away uneasily.

"Are you well enough to pull the sled now?" she asked, getting to her feet, the old stiffness returning to her voice. "Ramose will be angry if he returns to see that we have not moved."

Still avoiding her eyes, the slave stood.

Tetisheri hobbled to the sled, settling back onto it. The throbbing in her foot resumed, white hot.

Silently, the slave re-roped himself to the sled's handles and began to drag his burden through the sand.

Ramose waited and watched at the edge of the court-yard as Tetisheri finished her song. Nakht had thirteen other noblemen as guests this evening. They nodded appreciatively. In the weeks she'd been at the house, her lovely voice had grown stronger as her confidence had increased.

He was glad that he was stationed outside Luxor for the time being. It made it easy to come visit her. Nakht appreciated the service he had performed for him and made him welcome.

When she was finished, she bowed and limped from the courtyard. Her foot was nearly better, but she could not put her full weight on it. Ramose had brought her a cane with golden hieroglyphic engraving. She placed her hand on his arm and he guided her out to a bench in the garden.

"Your voice grows more beautiful every day," he complimented. She thanked him and he moved closer. "I will have to return to Nubia soon," he told her. "There are still pockets of rebels to be dealt with there. Before I go, I want to ask you to become my wife when I return."

She did not smile in delight as he had hoped.

"Why not decide this after you return?" she suggested.

Her evasiveness angered him and he stood, scowling. "Because I want to know your feelings right now," he insisted. He pulled a pouch from his sword belt and presented it her. "I have brought you this as a token of my pledge to you."

She opened the pouch into her palm. It was an Eye of Horus pendant on a golden cord. Within the turquoise eye was set a multifaceted glittering green emerald. "The jewel is from the emerald mines of the south," he told her.

From the admiring way she held the pendant, he could see how much she loved it. "Ramose, it is too beautiful," she murmured, clearly awestruck by the gift.

"It suits you."

She smiled lovingly down at the piece of green jewelry. But was the smile for him or his gift?

It had happened while Taharaq was feeding the geese. He had been told to cage one for the evening meal, and as he had seized it around the neck, the enraged goose nipped his hand hard.

A Nubian curse flew from his mouth as he pulled his hand back.

Sound.

The wound to his throat had healed.

Checking that there were no witnesses, he spoke a sentence in his native language. His voice was a low rasp — but it was a voice.

He closed his eyes to staunch tears of relief. This muteness had humiliated him. Now with a voice, he had acquired a secret weapon and he decided to keep it a secret. Better to be thought of as mute among these harsh people.

Feeling newly powerful, he grabbed the goose from behind. "I'm sorry," he whispered to it as he slipped a cord muzzle over its beak. "But we are both slaves and I have no choice."

Taharaq beheaded the goose and was bringing it into the kitchen when he noticed Nerfi idling near the chopping table, fingering the dinner linens absently. There was something about her he didn't trust. Perhaps it was that strange red wig, but he suspected it was more her darting black eyes that put him on guard whenever she was near.

"I have been waiting here to ask you something," she said in a sensuous, insinuating tone.

She glanced at old blind Seth who sat by the large baking oven, pounding on a round of dough. She nodded for Taharaq to follow her several feet farther away from him. "Do you want to go home?" she asked quietly.

His expression instantly registered interest in what she might propose, and she moved even closer to him. "I have met a boatman who will smuggle slaves back down the Nile. It will cost you. What have you to offer?"

Taharaq shook his head.

"I thought not," Nerfi continued. "This house is full of valuable things. See what you can steal and then signal to me. I will sell it for you and buy your passage home."

"I could go with you," she said, rubbing up against him. "We could both be free and you would have me by your side."

He saw what she was up to. She wanted him to risk stealing something valuable enough to buy them both passage to Nubia. If he got caught, it would be his hands on the chopping block, not hers. Once they were there she would no doubt desert him for a more prosperous suitor.

I am no thief, he thought contemptuously, *nor does your shallow allure tempt me.* It took all his discipline to keep silent.

Nerfi read his expression, however. "Or maybe you'd rather be a slave forever," she suggested silkily. "It's your decision."

Tetisheri limped into the kitchen, aided by her cane. Nerfi's eyes darted to the gorgeous green jeweled Eye of Horus she wore on a golden cord around her neck and then back to Taharaq.

He looked away.

"There you are, Nerfi," Tetisheri said pleasantly.

"Renenutet asks that you bring water to Nakht, who is in the study with his accounts." Nerfi grabbed a water pitcher and began to pump water into it.

"Your head, how does it feel?" Tetisheri asked.

Taharaq nodded. He had not had one of his blistering headaches since their trip through the desert. He gestured toward her foot.

"It is getting better each day. Soon I won't need this cane," she answered the silent question. "I do not know what the hieroglyphics on it mean. I can read a little but not enough to tell what this says."

He gestured for her to give it to him. Leaning against the nearby chopping table, she handed it over. A quick look was all he required to decipher it.

It was a story about the construction of the pyramids at Giza over a thousand years ago, and how the high priests had studied the night sky and arranged for the three pyramids to align with certain stars. It was a story that had always fascinated him. He wondered why they had done this. Was this some sort of landing guide for gods who descended to visit them at some time in the past? It was a mystery lost to antiquity, but one that the people still pondered.

How could he silently convey this to her?

He checked on Nerfi's whereabouts and found her hovering near the door with her jug, waiting to catch his eye. Seeing that she had it, she made a tiny but meaningful nod toward Tetisheri's pendant, and then departed.

When he and Tetisheri were at last free of Nerfi, his mind raced, wondering if he could share his secret of new speech with her. He still had not made a decision when his mouth opened and words came out. "It tells of the pyramids," he said with a quick glance at Seth, checking that the old man had not heard.

Mouth agape, Tetisheri stared at him.

He realized he had spoken in his own language. She had no idea what he'd told her, only that he'd spoken. Her amazement made him smile. "It returned just today," he explained softly, this time speaking in Egyptian.

She returned his smile. "You are healing."

He nodded. "Much better these days. Yes."

They stood together and he felt as though they were enveloped in an invisible web, as though the *ka* life force that surrounded each person had formed one *ka* now containing both of them.

She felt it, too. Her face was unmistakably soft as she gazed into his eyes, seeking out some part of him that was hidden. Whatever she sought, he longed to reveal it, just as strongly as his physical body craved the touch of her golden skin.

"I long to talk with you," she said softly. "You are so different from me, come from so far away. I want to know everything about you."

Together they walked into the garden.

Tetisheri grew to prize the time she spent with Taharaq in the garden. The mornings were particularly good for talking together because she did not perform until the evening.

She would rise early just to spend time with him as he tended the geese. He was careful to keep his back to the kitchen window as he spoke to her, careful to always be engaged in some chore. For her part, she worked on a silken wall-hanging that depicted cranes in flight. It gave her an excuse — she claimed she liked to sit out in the open air to work. It cleared her head, she said.

With these cautions in place, they spent pleasurable hours together every day. With Ramose away at war, she thought little of him and found that whenever her thoughts were not engaged on some task, it was Taharaq who came to mind.

Tetisheri was amazed by the things Taharaq could tell her. She'd never realized the Nubian culture was so rich. They had built pyramids before the Egyptians and had many more of them. It was the Egyptians who had learned from the Nubians.

"We call our people Te-Seti," he told her, using the Nubian phrase. He had his back to the kitchen window and was planting small palms in a row by the back wall. "It means *land of the bow*, since our people are proud of their skills as archers."

"And how did you learn to write so well?" she

murmured, looking intently at her wall-hanging, pretending to be focused on the stitches.

He explained that his father had been a scribe at the royal palace. He was training his son to do the same. Taharaq believed language was the most important skill a person could possess and had worked hard to learn. But this had been cut short when he'd joined the rebels.

"Nakht could use a scribe," she told him impulsively, putting down her craftwork, excited at the possibility. "It would not be as great as being a royal scribe, but Nakht is a rich and powerful man. Write something and I will show him."

He nodded, still with his back to her.

The life of a scribe would be infinitely better for him than the life of a slave. She could never think of marrying a slave . . . but a scribe . . .

One day, she noticed that his eyes were red, irritated. When she asked about it, he told her that they had been bothering him lately. Tetisheri took a tin of green eye kohl from the small bag at her waist. "Let me line your eyes with this," she offered. "It is the fashion, but it has a use. It contains ground copper, which protects against eye irritation."

"Is it fitting for a slave to wear?" he asked as he fed the geese in their pen.

She grunted disdainfully. "What does it matter? Besides, you are not a slave born and you will not be a slave long. This will make you look more Egyptian. I will tell Nakht tonight about your skill and training as a scribe. You will soon begin your new life out of slavery."

Ramose seethed as he watched them through the kitchen window. Blind Seth had told him this was going on, had been occurring the whole time he was away in Nubia. Blind Seth couldn't see, but his other senses more than made up for the lack.

Blind Seth hated him. He made no secret of this until Ramose had threatened to use his influence with Nakht to have him thrown out of the household as useless. Once Seth was good and afraid of him, he put him to use. The old man may have been an unlikely spy but he was an effective one. They were sitting exactly as he'd said they would be.

Still, he would have known it himself, even if Seth hadn't informed. The song she'd sung the night before — it was a Nubian song! He'd heard it himself at a festival while he was there. Where else could she have learned it but from the slave? And if he'd taught her a song, it meant he could speak! The night before he had been too furious at the song to stay, so she didn't yet know he had returned. But now he was here to settle this — and put an end to it.

A darkness of jealousy descended like a cloud of locust as he watched her apply liner to the slave's eyes. He sat right beside her on the bench! How gently, caressingly she worked.

Why did she touch him like that?

Ramose recalled the one time he had tried to take her into his arms. She had been stiff and turned her head away when he tried to kiss her. Her excuse had been that she was tired!

But now she was practically melting into this slave's arms! What did she find so delightful about a slave?

Looking up, Tetisheri saw him and jumped away from Taharaq, sending her kohl pot spinning onto the ground. She arose, a frantic expression blotting out the laughter she'd been sharing. With a quick word to the slave she hurried toward the kitchen.

"Is it appropriate for the household entertainer to fraternize with a slave?" He attacked the moment she came through the kitchen door. "It's bad enough that you associate with that servant girl. Have you no regard for your position in this household, or for mine? Is it your intention to make me the object of mockery?"

"Ramose, do not be angry," she began. "But we must talk."

"There are no words to excuse this," he insisted angrily. "You will not spend time with him anymore."

"I will speak to whom I please," she stated.

He grabbed her upper arm roughly, beyond caring if he harmed her. He did not tolerate insubordination among his men in the army and he would not take it from a woman. "He will be sent to the stone quarry this very morning and you will not see him ever again."

"Nakht will not allow it," she shouted.

"I will supply two new slaves to Nakht, fresh from Nubia. He will not stop me."

"You won't," she cried. "I won't let you!"

Yanking her up close to his face, he spoke in a threatening growl. "You have taken my gifts and thereby implied your consent to be my wife. I will not be made a fool of, do you hear me?"

Tetisheri tried to shake him off, but his hold was too firm. "You're hurting me," she shouted, struggling to push him away.

As she broke free of him, Ramose grabbed for her. He clutched the cord holding the pendant around her neck. The gold cord broke and it clattered onto the floor.

Tetisheri rushed out of the kitchen so he did not see, at first, that the slave had come into the doorway. And when he did turn to notice him, he held the image of the man's face for only the most fleeting of seconds before the rock-hard impact of the man's fist snapped his jaw.

Taharaq did not know if Ramose lay dead or simply passed out. He was certain, however, that if they caught him now his own death was assured.

It had been a rash, stupid thing to do. He'd acted on impulse when he heard Tetisheri cry out.

But, staring down at Ramose, he felt as if it was an act that had been inevitable, and he was deeply satisfied.

He knew his satisfaction would be brief if he was caught.

The kitchen was empty, but in a minute someone was bound to enter. His eyes lit on Tetisheri's bejeweled Eye of Horus pendant gleaming there on the floor. Scooping it into his hand, he dashed back out into the garden.

Keeping close to the house, he moved quickly around the back. It was not difficult to climb to the top of the garden wall.

He could make his way into Luxor and find the boatman Nerfi had spoken of. He had the pendant for payment. But the man Nerfi had told him of would be nearly impossible to inquire about without calling attention to himself, and they would be searching for him. He had to find Nerfi somehow. She had to help him find the boatman.

Crouching low atop the stone wall, he peered out onto the palm-lined road running in front of the house. A trader trudged beside two camels loaded with bundles, most likely on his way to Luxor. That was the way; if he stayed off the road, he could follow it into the city.

He dropped to the ground on the far side, flattening himself against the outside wall of the house. Tetisheri's room was not far. If he had luck, she would be there. She could summon Nerfi for him.

Would Tetisheri go with him?

No, it was too dangerous.

He couldn't ask it of her. He would return for her. He would tell her to wait for him. He would become a scribe like his father before him. He would come back as a man of means who she could be proud to wed.

Amun-Ra scorched the sky from the highest point. "Great Amun-Ra," he prayed, "keep me alive in Tetisheri's heart. Allow me to return to her on time's swiftest wings."

From the kitchen, a woman screamed.

Ramose had been discovered.

The news of Taharaq's escape reached Tetisheri as she sat in her room stroking her small cub. Nerfi rushed in to report that he had broken the strong jaw of which Ramose was so proud, but Ramose was now up and on the hunt.

"He's wild with rage," Nerfi told Tetisheri in a rush of frantic words. "His face is swollen and raw and he doesn't seem to even feel the pain. He's out of his mind."

Fear gripped Tetisheri, squeezing her around the chest, cutting off her breath. Putting the cub aside, she reached up and laid her hand on the mural of Isis for support. "Help me, Mother, what should I do?" she implored.

Her green Eye of Horus pendant was suddenly flung up onto the sill of her open window.

Her eyes darted to the image of Isis and then to Taharaq, who had climbed into the window, pendant now again in his hand.

Tetisheri didn't understand. What was he doing there?

He suddenly cried out, an anguished howl of pain. Then he plummeted to the floor, a sword plunged into his chest.

She recognized the sword's ornate handle instantly.

Whirling around, Tetisheri faced Ramose. He was terrifying in his fury, his eyes burning madly, his right cheek swollen to twice its size. His chest heaved with the effort of hurling his sword with such force that it had pierced Taharaq clear through.

"You will hang," he snarled at Nerfi in a muffled growl. "Smuggling slaves is a high crime."

"I wasn't," Nerfi protested, trembling.

"Blind Seth heard you tell him to steal the pendant for payment. He came here just now to give it to you. You saw it yourself."

Ramose pried the pendant from Taharaq's fingers and faced Tetisheri. "He attacked me for it after you left the kitchen."

With a flick of his finger, he set the Eye of Horus spinning on its cord. A shard of sunlight flashed the lights from its multifaceted emerald around the walls.

Ramose grabbed Nerfi under her armpit, lifting her onto her toes, and dragged her, white-faced with fear, toward the door, tossing her toward two of his men. "Lock her in her room. I will see to her later."

The kohl that rimmed Tetisheri's eyes ran in two black rivers down her face as, with one hand, he turned and shoved her against the back wall. "These two slaves will disappear and we will forget this ever came between us," he mumbled thickly.

"I will never marry you!" she shrieked at him. "I will go to the temple of Isis and become a priestess there!"

"I will see you dead before that happens," Ramose replied as he left.

Tetisheri let herself slide slowly down until she sat beside Taharaq. How could she have loved this man? He had stolen from her. He had intended to leave her there to face Ramose alone.

And she had believed, had been convinced beyond doubt, that she loved him.

She had been so wrong about him.

And, despite it all, she loved him still.

Tetisheri hugged herself and slowly began to rock back and forth. A humming came from a place within her that she had not known existed, and yet it was strangely familiar. The humming rose slowly, transforming itself into an anguished wail.

Then

The cry of sorrow fills the chamber. My beloved is so distraught that she does not realize that I have my arms around her. *Do not wail so, dearest love, I am beside you.*

I stroke her lovely black hair but the aggrieved howl streaming from her lips will not abate.

What can be the cause of such sorrow?

My eyes rest on the body of a man. *My brother, Aken, has been slain!*

Alarmed, I leave my sobbing dear one and go to his side.

Soldiers come to lift Aken.

Tetisheri throws herself on his body, screaming at them not to take him, drenching his blood-smeared chest with her tears.

I do not understand.

Does she love Aken?

I did not know she had ever met him. But she must have known him. Why else would he have been here in her room? Perhaps he had escaped the stone quarry and come to free me — and been caught.

Tetisheri, what has happened here?

She gives no sign of having heard me.

Answer me, my love.

She can hold back the soldiers no longer and they carry Aken from the room. I follow, needing to be sure they prepare his body correctly for the afterlife, despite the fact that they despise him as a slave. Trailing them through the house, I stay near as they travel down to the banks of the Nile with Aken's body draped between them.

My heart aches to think of my young brother, lying dead, his hand lifelessly trailing in the dirt.

I am overcome with horror as I realize what is about to happen. There will be no preparation of his body.

With not even a prayer to Osiris, his body is flung into the Nile. The soldiers turn back without a second glance, but I stand there on the riverbank watching as he floats back to the surface, face down. A small wave created by a passing barge pushes him over.

I see his face.

And at once I know the truth that my heart had been denying.

It is not Aken who has died.

It is I who am dead.

A crocodile appears in the water, gliding toward the body, and I turn away, unable to look.

So I am stranded there, unprepared to move to the Next World, the one that those with greater means have so thoroughly planned for.

I find that my movement in the world is swift, requiring little more than thought. In a blink, I return to Nubia once more to brush my mother's coarse, black hair, to kiss her beloved forehead. Her two sons are gone and she is perpetually sad. My deceased father has left some valuables buried under the house. He has written the whereabouts on a tablet. My mother has it but can't read it. She is afraid to ask anyone for help in fear that someone will steal her treasure. My father expected me to decipher it for her, and now I do, breathing the location into her ear. My mother thinks the information has come to her on the desert wind — and perhaps it has.

I visit Aken in the quarry. With an invisible hand, I help him carry his load.

But how much longer can my *ka* exist in this state? I am weakening already, though I experience no need for food, drink, or sleep.

Lost and confused, I roam the Valley of the Kings, thinking I might find the things I need in those great pyramids and tombs. When I go in, effortlessly passing through the massive walls, the wealth within staggers even my wildest imaginings.

Deep in the confines of one underground tomb, I meet a ruler, a hundred years dead, though not more than twenty years of age — the boy pharaoh Tutankhamen, son of Akhenaton. He is rummaging through the many things that had been stored there for his use. *I am searching for my lute*, he tells me. *I am bored and desire to play.*

I ask if he will take me to the Next World, but he says that Osiris, who rules there, would not allow it, not without the correct burial.

Desire to be reborn, he advises. *Try again.*

But how? I ask.

He shrugs, finding his lute in a golden case. *You must surrender your love of this world, I suppose. Allow it to happen. Wish it to happen. Picture it in your mind.*

I would not be a slave, I say. *I would live a carefree life, free of ambition or desire.*

Then think hard on this desire, Tutankhamen advises as his image fades from my view.

A mummy case in the corner of the tomb begins to glow with a vivid white light. The case grows until it is many feet tall. A strange hum emanates from within it.

I approach, irresistibly drawn to the light-filled case, and enter the light.

(On the Wheel of Rebirth)

Pakistan, 538 B.C.E.:

Today I came upon a young man lying on the Peshawar road. I had met him in a friend's home the evening before. His companion was a man who seemed of noble birth though roughly dressed. Clearly they had both been traveling a long time. His friend's name was Guatama Siddhartha. The two companions had already had too much wine when they began to argue over the nature of the soul. This Siddhartha believed that the soul perished along with the body. My young nameless friend would have none of it, disagreeing vehemently. "The soul lives on and on!" he declared.

"How do you know?" Siddhartha asked.

"I don't know how I know. I just know," the drunken, nameless one insisted.

"Perhaps we are saying the same thing and it is only the nature of earthly time that eludes us," this Siddhartha allowed, desiring to smooth the argument and make peace, I believe.

The nameless one shook his head. "No. I think not."

"Perhaps one continues to be reborn depending on how one has behaved — for good or bad — in the previous life.

One will continue to do this until all issues have been resolved or understood and then one can cease to exist and move on to the bliss of Nirvana," Siddhartha explained.

The man whose name I did not know drained my friend's wine jug into his flask and sucked it in. "I don't understand anything you say these days," he slurred.

"We have been drinking and carousing too much," Siddhartha said. "But when I tried to fast in order to become holy, I nearly died of starvation. I have been thinking that there must be a middle way, a way that avoids the extremes of self-denial as well as the extremes of earthly pleasure."

"Get out of here!" my nameless friend bellowed. "You're no fun anymore. You've gotten too serious. You're making my headaches come back."

With a bow, Siddhartha left.

"Go!" the nameless one shouted after him. "Go sit under a bodhi tree for the rest of your life, for all I care."

Not much afterward, my rowdy friend staggered out into the night alone, clutching his flask of wine.

This morning I found him on the side of the road. I thought him dead and stepped closer. His robe was askew and at first I thought he had been run through at the side with a sword or spear. On closer inspection I realized it was a purple birthmark in the shape of an awful gash.

I jumped back in surprise when he lifted his head and greeted me. I have never seen a happier grin on any man.

Athens, 415 B.C.E.:

Luck be with you, Artem, my son. May the gods and goddesses of Mount Olympus bestow you with blessings. I leave you here with this note on your blanket, on this sea-thrown rock.

It may be that you will die here, but I would rather this than that you be born into slavery. I am a slave from Egypt sold here to Greece, the land that now rules my home. You are a son of Egypt but your father is a freeborn citizen here in Athens. He knows not whether you are boy or girl, only that you should be put out as not to bring disgrace.

Sewn into your blanket are these green peridot earrings brought from an island in the Red Sea. They have been in my family for all time, passed on from one generation to the next. They are all I have of wealth. Trade them well if you must, for they have value.

Good-bye, my little one, my Artem.

Athens, 399 B.C.E.

Hyacinth stood on her marble balcony, eyes intent on the spot in the woods where she'd seen the stranger emerge at sunset the day before. Tucking a loose strand of wavy brown hair into the golden cord that held her hair back, she studied the tree line for signs of movement.

Her eyes wandered over to the rocky Aegean Sea coast at the left of the woods. The dull roar of its pounding surf drifted toward her on the breeze. It was there that he'd gone yesterday after he shot the hare, and later a duck, with his arrow.

She still thought of him as the wild boy. Though it was clear enough from the glimpse she'd caught of him the other day that he'd grown into a young man.

There he was.

The orange trail of Apollo's descending sun chariot outlined the wild boy's tight, black curls as he stepped from the woods. His white tunic showed off a leanly muscular physique. She remembered his strikingly black, almond-shaped eyes from the times she'd seen him before.

Hyacinth hurried down the side steps, lifting her long, tan tunic dress so it wouldn't trip her. A dull pain in her right foot abruptly slowed her, throwing her onto the railing for support.

Breathing out in exasperation, disgusted at her lameness, she cursed the weak foot that had, since birth, turned under at the most critical moments. More than once, while dancing or running, it had mortified her by bringing her crashing to her knees. No physician could account for it other than to say it was perhaps a curse from the gods for some sin of her parents.

Rubbing the offending foot, she set out at a slower pace, keeping along the edges of the wide yard that ended in acres of thick woods. Her father kept it uncultivated so he and Hyacinth's two older brothers could hunt. Her parents had forbidden her to go too far, considering the woods unsafe for a girl.

Still, the woods weren't wholly unfamiliar to her, since she was not, by nature, inclined toward obedience. Now she picked her way through the sun-flecked trees, taking care with her bad foot, coming ever closer to the young man who had been the wild boy.

His name was Artem. She knew because she had heard it years ago at the marketplace. He had been picking through a pig trough, looking for food, when first she saw him.

"Never you mind about him," her slave woman, Charis, had chided roughly when she'd noticed Hyacinth studying the boy.

"But why must he eat among the pigs?" Hyacinth had asked.

Charis turned her attention to the fish laid out on the iced table before her, searching for the freshest catch. "He's trash, no doubt abandoned by some slave," she replied as she lifted a small octopus and stretched its tentacle to examine. "He'll be scooped up and sold into slavery himself sometime soon. Mark my words. That's what happens to such as he."

Artem had looked up from the trough and had walked toward them, almost as if he had sensed he was the subject of their discussion. Hyacinth straightened her posture, brushed back her long curls, and resolved to know him better.

She tilted her head in confusion as he walked by her without even a glance.

Nadim, the fish seller, scooped an eel from the iced table and tossed it to him. Its silvery, snakelike body twisted as it sailed through the air. "Here's supper for you, my young friend."

With a delighted laugh, the boy caught it.

"The men have a fire out back, Artem. Tell them I said to cook it up for you," Nadim added.

The eel undulated in his hand but Artem held tight, observing it merrily. He noticed that Hyacinth was keenly studying the eel, so he thrust the creature at her, intent on watching a young girl scream in disgusted terror.

Determined not to show the expected weakness, Hyacinth instead reached forward to pat the creature on the head.

Artem's upper lip quirked into a grudging smile, and she knew she'd won his respect.

Since that day, Artem had been in her head. The idea of living by her own wits, as he did, inflamed her imagination. It thrilled her when she caught sight of him in the street or at the market. As the years passed, she began to think of him as attractive.

He was newly in her mind because she'd caught sight of him in the square not long ago. And then, suddenly, he had appeared — practically in her own backyard.

Her heart had leaped excitedly, so glad to see that although he was a thief, poaching a hare on her father's land, he was not yet a slave. Now that he had appeared again this day, as she'd hoped he would; she was determined to speak to him, to learn what his life was like.

At the seaward edge of the woods, she caught sight of him again, moving toward the gently sloping, rocky shore. Reaching up for a branch, she hoisted herself onto it, shimmying out onto the limb for a better view.

His bow was drawn and aimed. Looking skyward, she spotted his target. A fat gull descended to the shoreline for its supper of fish.

His arrow whistled through the air and struck the bird

while it was still in flight. The gull plummeted from the sky into the ocean surf.

He disappeared from view as he ran to claim his prey. Curious, she crawled farther onto her branch, straining to see where he'd gone.

Minutes passed as she waited for him to re-emerge.

He did not appear again, and she began to worry. Had Poseidon pulled him under?

More time passed, and still he did not return.

She had pushed herself up to get a better view when something clamped on to her right foot. Crying out in surprise, she tumbled from the tree, falling on top of Artem. The two of them landed on the ground, the dead gull he held sliding into the leaves.

"Let me go!" she demanded.

He laughed and held tight.

Lunging onto his hand with both of hers, she struggled to pry his fingers loose. "Let go, I say!" The pain in her right foot flared again. "Ow!" she shouted.

At this, he released her, jumping back. "Are you all right?"

"No! Oh, it's not your fault — not *all* your fault, anyway. This cursed foot always gives me trouble!" She looked up at him sharply. "What did you do that for?"

"Spies should be prepared to be caught," he said lightly, getting to his feet.

"You're trespassing, you know," she said, merely to regain some dignity as she hopped to her feet. With her weight on her left, she smoothed her skirt.

"I have not poached on your father's land," he defended himself. "The gull was in the air and therefore belonged to any hunter."

"Yesterday you poached."

His eyes narrowed. "How long have you been watching me?"

She simply shrugged. "Long enough. You are Artem, the wild boy," she said.

He laughed with a bit of scorn. "So I'm called. Aren't you frightened that I might rip you to shreds and devour you?"

She shook her head. "I've seen you before. And I saw you in the town square not long ago. You were listening to that old philosopher speak."

"Socrates. I could listen to that old man speak forever. Never have I heard words spoken with such eloquence and such intelligence."

"You speak quite eloquently yourself," she pointed out. "Who taught you?"

"The sailors down at the docks, mostly."

"I've never heard sailors to be known for their eloquence," she commented.

This made him laugh. "No, you're right. I've learned words from them I would never repeat in your presence. They can be a rough group. What I meant was that some of them know how to read and write, and through the years one or another of them has taught me. Once I could read, I taught myself by reading anything I could. And, as you say, I love to listen to the philosophers in the square."

She pointed to a scroll tucked into the belt of his tunic. "Is that one of the things you read?" she asked.

He pulled the scroll out and handed it to her, but she shook her head, waving it away. "I wish I could read, but my father believes education is wasted on a girl."

"That's a shame," he sympathized. "Though I realize it is the common opinion, it's a stupid one."

"I would like to learn to read," she admitted for the first time in her life. To have said this to anyone else would have been to invite scorn and ridicule so she never said it, barely allowed herself to think it. He was so different from everyone else, though. She felt that she had always known him and could trust him with her most secret thoughts. It made no sense and yet the feeling was so strong.

"You should learn," he said. "I will teach you if no one else will."

"Would you?" she checked eagerly.

He nodded. "I don't like the idea of anyone being kept down, especially you."

"Why especially me?" she asked, surprised by her own boldness.

A flush of color came to his cheeks. "Because you're not a silly girl. You deserve to learn."

"How can you tell?" she asked.

"I just know," he murmured quietly. "We can start with this. It's a copy of a work by Herodotus the historian. It is his description of life in ancient Egypt. Though Greece rules Egypt now, it hasn't always been the case. It's very interesting to read about their old culture. I am told my mother was of Egyptian descent, though I never knew her."

"I can see the Egyptian in you, just a bit," she said.

"We'll read it together," he agreed. "Let me put this bird down first."

She trailed him into the woods until they came to a campsite. There he gutted his gull and tied it upside down from a tree. "Is this where you live?" she asked.

"I live wherever is convenient," he told her. "When you have no home it's easy to move as soon as you're discovered."

"Don't you want a home?" she questioned.

"I don't want anything other than to live each day as it comes. To want things is to be constantly disappointed."

"You don't want a job or a family?"

"Definitely not a job," he said with a laugh. "Any job is a form of slavery. You toil and labor like Hercules . . . and for what? A few drachmas and an early death?"

"Why are you so concerned about slavery?" she asked him. "You are not a slave."

"Aren't *you* concerned about it?" he countered. "A woman in Athens is a man's slave with no rights, no freedoms."

Hyacinth laughed with scorn. "I do not toil or labor like a slave. In fact, I do just about nothing all day. I would almost rather be a slave."

"You're a silly girl to say that," he scolded. For the first time, she sensed disapproval from him, and was sorry for it. She remembered Charis telling her that he was the child of a slave and could be dragged into slavery himself. How foolish she must have sounded to him.

"House slaves do all right," he went on, "but in the mines and quarries slaves know only a life of grueling toil with no respite."

"I suppose you're right." She was eager to change the subject, realizing that she had sounded shallow and probably stupid to him. "Tell me what you have learned about ancient Egypt."

Artem sat beside her on a flat rock and unrolled the scroll. "I'll point to the words as I read," he said. "That way you'll get the sense of how the written words and the spoken words line up. It's how I began to learn," he said.

Hyacinth was fascinated as he read the words of Herodotus to her. According to the Greek historian, many of the customs the Greeks thought of as their own had actually been brought back to Greece by travelers to Egypt. He claimed that even their gods and goddesses were simply versions of the Egyptian gods, that the Greek goddess of fertility, Demeter, was the same as the Egyptian goddess Isis, but only by another name, and Dionysus was known in Egypt as Osiris. "Do you know that they had gods and goddesses who were half animal and half human, like Anubis the dog-headed god? They had two goddesses who were both half cat, half woman. They were named Bast and Sempket," he told her. "It's similar to our Pan, and the other centaurs."

"I heard that they worshipped cats. I have recently been given an African wildcat," she mentioned. "My father received it from a merchant sailor who brought it on a ship from Egypt. I've named it Baby and love it so much."

"Herodotus mentions the wildcats," Artem told her, finding it in his text. "The first ones were brought here when Alexander the Great conquered Egypt."

Herodotus described so much: the clothing, the ceremonies, the daily life of the average Egyptian, as well as the ways of the pharaohs. Artem paused in his reading and looked up from the scroll. "He writes so well. Somehow I can just see it all so clearly."

Hyacinth nodded enthusiastically. "I feel as if I am right there."

"It's true," he agreed.

"You read well," she added. "Do you really aspire to no position in life?"

"Maybe one thing, though it sounds so foolish, you'll laugh."

"Tell," she urged. She enjoyed seeing him less than sure about something.

"I have started a few poems," he admitted sheepishly.

"Not an epic like that told by Homer, telling of war and heroism, gods and monsters. My poems are about nature and its beauty. Sometimes I write about Artemis, the goddess of the hunt, whom I was named for."

"Who named you?" she asked.

"I was found with a note pinned to me," he revealed. "A slave woman who had been freed by her dead master found me and raised me until she died five years later. I don't mind being named for the goddess, since she was the greatest archer."

"Just like you," Hyacinth noted.

"I've always had skill with a bow," he admitted.

His upper lip quirked into the slightest smile. It reminded her of the way he'd smiled at her that day in the fish market. She could see he was pleased that she'd remarked on his skill. He seemed proud of it, which meant *something* mattered to him, at least. So she continued. "You could compete in the Olympic Games with skill such as yours. I believe there's some sort of prize. It might improve your . . . situation."

"Archery seems a blessing Artemis has bestowed on me as her namesake," he mused aloud. "I have been able to shoot with great accuracy since I was quite small and have never really had an instructor. You've given me an interesting idea, though. Perhaps the Olympic Games are something I should look into. After all, they give honor to the gods of Olympus and it might please Artemis."

"Plus, you could use the prize to better your station in life," she repeated. "You must want some comforts."

He laughed. "The Spartans don't believe in comforts. They think it weakens the mind and soul."

"Yes, but we are not Spartans," she replied.

"No, and nor would I want to be. You're right. I wouldn't mind the funds to buy a few of life's good things," he admitted. He looked up at her, realizing something. "What's *your* name? You haven't told me."

"Hyacinth."

"Ah, a lovely flower," he said softly, looking at her hard as if trying to really see her. She wanted him to see her, longed to reveal to him all that was beneath her surface. And in the same way, she wanted to dig behind his exterior to the person she could sense was there beneath.

She felt engulfed by his gaze and was seized with the idea that their faces, their skins, were disguises. If they could only pull them off somehow, the real people inside would be revealed and these two souls would recognize each other instantly and love each other deeply.

It was crazy, maybe, but she was sure it was true.

The scroll rolled from his lap, breaking the tension of their gazes.

"Once you have learned to read," he said, bending to retrieve the scroll, "they'll all wonder how you know so much. I'd love to see their astonished faces when you know everything books can teach you." He laughed at the idea, and his eyes shone. "Don't worry. I'll make sure you learn."

His promise had been to teach her to read but she felt that it meant so much more. "I'll teach you to read" meant he would cherish her, want the best for her, be her companion as she came to know the world. Hyacinth was as sure of this as if he had sworn it to her. She heard it in his warm tone, saw it in the smile on his face when he looked at her. And it filled her with love for him.

He was the one for her. She just knew.

There was nothing to it, now, but to confess what she had been thinking. Until this moment, the thought had stayed hidden in the back of her mind. Only now did she realize it had been there all along. She angled herself away so she would not have to look at him directly.

"I'll be fourteen soon," she began, "and my father is holding a contest of athletic skill in order to choose a husband for me."

"Do you desire a husband?" he asked.

"No," she replied. "If I could choose my destiny, I would go serve Athena in her temple as a priestess. A priestess of Athena is taught to read the sacred stories of the gods and goddesses. She serves a higher purpose than catering to her husband, as I will be forced to do if I marry."

"Then I would never want to compete for your hand in marriage," he said.

"But my father will not hear of me becoming a priest-ess," she clarified quickly. "And since I *must* marry, I would rather it be to someone with whom I am companionable. Marriage could be an agreeable thing, perhaps, if one found a soul mate."

"A what?"

"I, too, heard the philosopher Socrates speak in the square once. He believes we are part physical and mortal, and part soul, the part which lives on after death. I started thinking: If one could find a mate with whom one might travel companionably through all time in love and under-standing, then . . ."

She cut herself off, feeling foolish.

"Then what?" he prompted.

"Then a person might really find happiness."

"And you think this can happen through marriage?" he asked.

"With the right mate. If one is lucky."

Once again, their eyes met and something passed between them that she could not name. It was attraction, yes, but also recognition. There was something in him that made her want to stay beside him, to curl her head onto his chest with never the thought of leaving.

She stepped toward him but he broke the connec-tion, tossing it away with a harsh laugh. "I am a homeless scrounger," he reminded her.

"I have a large dowry. My father is a wealthy importer and exporter of goods."

She could hardly believe these words were coming from her. How shameful to be begging a complete stranger to vie for her hand in marriage! But all the young men who would come to compete for her would be strangers as well, and some much older and not nearly as good-looking. If she would be wed to a stranger, then let it be Artem — Artem, whom she barely knew but who did not feel like a stranger to her. She knew she'd be happy married to this person she had felt she knew on that very first day when she'd spied him in the fish market. Of course, it made no sense — but there it was, just the same.

He stood and waved her away. "No, I could never wed a siren."

"A what?"

He turned toward her. There was mischief in his eyes though his face was serious. "I have heard you down by the ocean rocks, singing into the crashing surf."

"You have?"

"Yes," he replied. "And I believe you must be a siren, one of the magical half-fish women who drive sailors mad with their song. Surely you've read of it in the work of the poet Homer?"

She had heard the tale told. She lifted her long, tan, linen skirt to reveal two sturdy legs. "No fish tail here," she said.

"I see. Those are most assuredly legs," he said as he smiled and his eyes ran appreciatively up and down the length of her body. "Then, tell me, how do you come to sing so enchantingly?"

Hyacinth was proud of her voice and it pleased her that she'd been overheard. Singing was the only thing she had ever been allowed to study despite the fact that her two older brothers were schooled in many subjects.

"I have a teacher," she told him. "He assigns me to sing over the crashing of the waves in order to strengthen my voice."

Artem pulled a scroll from under his roll of blankets beside the ashen remains of a fire. Then he took out a flute. "Sing this," he suggested. "It's a poem I wrote. I want to put music to accompany it. I have a plan that perhaps I can earn my keep playing and reciting my work in the homes of the wealthy."

"I can't read it," she reminded him.

"I'll recite it to you. Maybe you can remember it." He began to recite from memory. It was a poem telling of a trip up the Nile River taken by a slave being transported to Thebes, the city that had once been called Luxor before the Greeks renamed it.

Hyacinth was awestruck by the beauty of the language. It described the majesty of the pyramids and the slave's amazement in passing the great Sphinx for the first time.

He told of the slave wishing he could lift into the sky like a graceful crane and return to his homeland.

The pain and loneliness in the verses caused tears to well in Hyacinth's eyes. "How do you know such ancient things?" she asked when he was finished. "You are not singing of the Egypt that we Greeks rule. It is a much older Egypt that you sing of. Your words are so clear that I see it in my mind's eye. Why would you write of the life of a slave, you who are not tethered to anything?"

"I do not know why these images come to me. Sometimes the muses send pictures to me by day and other times Morpheus appears in my dreams and leads me to wondrous visions I cannot explain."

"Perhaps I have traveled there with you," she suggested.

He smiled, a bit bemused but not scornful. "Perhaps it is a thing akin to the Myth of Er that Plato refers to in his work *The Republic*."

Hyacinth had heard Plato's name discussed in the evenings when her father, brothers, and friends sat drinking their wine and debating issues she did not fully understand. But she had no idea about *The Republic* or the Myth of Er. Still, she could not bear for him to think her a fool. "Perhaps it *is* like the Myth of Er," she agreed.

"You'll read it for yourself someday," he said. "Can you remember the words to the poem?"

"Tell it to me again and this time I will listen closely

with a mind to recall it," she suggested, closing her eyes to concentrate.

Macar glanced around the gymnasium, checking that he was clear to throw, and then drew back his arm, hurling the javelin with all the force at his command.

Under his breath, he hissed a curse. The javelin had landed a full yard short of the farthest javelin thrown by Elpinor.

He rubbed his jaw. It was aching, as it often did when something worried him. Perhaps he'd been grinding his teeth in his sleep again, fretting about the upcoming tournament for Hyacinth's hand in marriage.

Elpinor slapped him on the back. "Have no worries. *I'm* not about to vie for my sister's hand in marriage, so you'll get no competition from me," he said, laughing. "Though why you would want her at all confounds me."

"I can't resist a contest," Macar joked glibly. "Besides, I hear she comes with an impressive dowry."

"That she does," Elpinor confirmed. "But is it worth putting up with such a sour disposition? Somehow she has no concept of the rightful place of a woman. She is forever listening in on the dialogues among the men, forever having to be shooed away like an intrusive hen."

Macar laughed even more loudly as he and Elpinor retrieved their javelins. "Perhaps it's simply that she's so disinterested in me," he pondered. "I relish the challenge.

Other girls are forever flirting with me. I'm considered quite a good catch. But your sister simply turns away when she sees me, almost as though I've done something to her."

"Your sin is being male," Elpinor told him. "If she had her way she'd join the priestesses in the temple and devote her life to Athena."

"That would be a waste of beauty," Macar commented, thinking of Hyacinth's attractive curves.

"My father forbids it, so there will be no waste of her beauty," Elpinor said. "But, I tell you, she will try your patience."

"I can subdue her," Macar insisted confidently. "After all, she is but a female."

Artem sat beside his campfire. It snapped as the flames danced, devouring the brittle branch he'd thrown onto it. It brought to mind the wild women at a bacchanalian feast.

He had taken his bow from his sack and removed an arrow from its quiver. Lying with the back of his head resting on a flat rock, he fit the arrow into the notch in the bow, aimed toward the fat, full moon, and waited.

A bat soared across its silvery path.

The arrow hissed through the darkness, taking down the creature.

Rising lazily, he strolled to where it had fallen and retrieved it. Not much meat on this, but he'd been so involved in working on his Egyptian poem this evening that he'd forgotten to hunt for his dinner.

He still had some figs he'd swiped from a nearby grove of trees. It would be enough.

He gutted the bat, pouring its blood into an earthenware cup. He had heard that drinking bat's blood could make a man invisible — a good quality to have when hunting. Then he set the bat on a spit over the fire.

Lost in thought, mesmerized once again by the fire, he absently plucked the taut string of his bow.

He could win her.

That he had the ability was never in question.

He wanted her. He had seen her from afar for years and thought her lovely, but when she approached him two days ago and he spoke to her, he felt the uncanny connection between them. It was surely something deeper than physical attraction.

She could not return to see him until tomorrow because she was committed to stand on a stool in the sewing chamber and be fitted for her wedding gown. He could picture her in it, the sun shining through crisp white lines; somehow he pictured her wearing a simple golden band around her forehead instead of the traditional wreath of hyacinths and violets. It would suit her better, in his opinion.

How much he longed to be the groom standing beside her. It was true that they had known each other but a day.

Yet it was a day with such a timeless quality: He felt as if he'd known her always.

But wanting things led to disaster. He had always been of this mind, although he was not sure why or wherefore he had come to this conclusion. Perhaps it was simply that as a person of no standing in the community he knew that nothing was coming to him. So why try?

Artem took a flask of wine from his sack, drawing in a long gulp. He was not meant to accomplish anything, to have anything. He had eluded the fates by avoiding slavery. That he was yet a free man should be enough for him. Why long for a life that was not his destiny to possess?

Once again he drank from the flask.

He did not intend to get yoked into the captivity of marriage. Lovely as she was, she would soon turn demanding, reminding him constantly that all they owned in the world had come from her dowry. He couldn't really imagine her being like this, but generally it seemed to be the way things went.

Then again ... he had thought about competing in the upcoming Olympic Games even before she'd brought it up. Perhaps with the winnings and status from an Olympic victory their positions would be more equal. . . .

No. It was too improbable an idea.

He had not eluded one kind of slavery simply to be tricked into another.

When she came to see him tomorrow as they'd arranged, he would not be there.

Closing his eyes, he tilted his head back and emptied the flask.

Perhaps I drink too much, he considered.

Hyacinth vowed to find out what he'd meant about the Myth of Er. She had asked her mother first, while she stood on a stool modeling her half-finished wedding garment. "I know not and neither do you need to know of such things," her mother chided as she pinned the white skirt into careful pleats. "You should be sewing this yourself. I hope your new husband won't notice that you can't embroider or weave, either, if you sing to him all the while."

"Perhaps if I knew how to create a clay vessel on the wheel he would be impressed," Hyacinth said. She had always wanted to learn the art of making pottery. The grace of its forms appealed to her. It would be lovely to create such beauty from wet clay, she thought.

"Pottery is not suitable as women's work, and you know that," her mother scoffed. "Now stand still!"

Later in the day, she tried to ask her father, but he was too busy to discuss anything with her. "I have ships coming into port in two days, the day of your wedding competition," he said absently as he pored over a wide ledger of accounts. "On them will be enough goods to restore your dowry."

"Restore?" she inquired.

He sputtered and his embarrassment showed. Apparently he had not intended to tell her this. "I had to borrow against it to pay a debt, but it's a temporary measure. The goods that are on those incoming ships will return full value to the fund."

When she asked her eldest brother Agapenor, he told her that girls shouldn't bother themselves about such things. So now, as a last resort, she would ask her other brother Elpinor who was two years older than she but, in her opinion, acted like a ten-year-old.

"What's the Myth of Er?" Hyacinth asked Elpinor at lunch the next day.

Elpinor stared at her quizzically, as though he hadn't understood the question. "Where did you hear of such things?" he asked. It wasn't the question that he didn't understand but the fact that it was she who had asked it that had stunned him.

He still hadn't answered when Macar came in to join them for lunch. "She wants to know what the Myth of Er is," Elpinor told his friend.

Macar didn't understand. "What use does she have for Plato?" he asked.

"Perhaps he can give her wedding advice!" Elpinor shouted, laughing.

"Toad," Hyacinth insulted her brother disgustedly.

Macar shrugged as he sat cross-legged against another bolster at the table. At least he wasn't a total fool like

Elpinor. Still, Macar's smug confidence made her dislike him immensely. She wished she didn't dislike him so much because he was the most likely suitor to win her father's contest.

"I remember learning about the Myth of Er," Macar suddenly recalled. "It's a nonsense story."

"What is it?" Hyacinth dared ask.

"Oh, it's crazy. It's about a fellow named Er who comes back from the dead. He's the only one who returns. He says the rest of the people who died went on to live in other bodies. Instead of living forever happily in the underworld ruled by Hades, God of the Dead — as all sane people know happens after they die — Plato thinks you go to some field and take a number like you might in the marketplace. Then when your number is called, you get to come back to this world in another body."

"Another body!" Elpinor shrieked with laughter. "Imagine! I'm drowned at sea and the next time I open my eyes someone is wiping my bare behind and feeding me baby slop!" Gales of laughter shook him.

"I don't think it sounds so funny," Hyacinth commented. It struck her as infinitely more interesting than endless days spent lolling around in some dull underworld.

"You're right!" Elpinor roared. "It's not funny, it's hilarious!"

Macar bit down on a smile as he reached toward a plate of dried apricots and nuts on the table. "Leave her alone.

Women are prone to such flights of fancy and childlike fantasy," he remarked. "It's perfectly normal."

Hot anger began to rise within Hyacinth, coloring her cheeks. "Plato was not a woman."

Macar chortled. "No, but he must have been dead drunk when he came up with that one."

Elpinor turned nearly purple with laughter at Macar's remark.

Hyacinth stared at Macar, narrowing her eyes angrily. Surely she could not be expected to marry this smug, condescending fool.

She *had* to convince Artem to compete for her. It was her only chance.

Casting a disdainful glance at Macar and her still-cackling brother, she hurried from the room and out to the balcony where she descended the side steps. Hurrying to the woods, she found Artem packing up his campsite. "You're not leaving?" she cried, alarmed by what she was seeing.

"Is it so important?" he asked lightly.

"Yes!" she insisted urgently. "You must compete for me."

"We hardly know each other," he protested.

"I know you better than any of the others. I know you better than Macar, who is my brother's friend. He comes to the house but I barely speak to him, and when I do, I am repulsed. You like me. I can tell you do. You promised to teach me to read!"

"I know Macar," he said. "He has often taunted me, calling me 'orphan of a slave.'"

"You don't like him any more than I do."

"No. Not much," he agreed.

"Then fight for me," she urged. "Don't let him win me."

Macar had trailed Hyacinth from the house. He could see she was angry with her brother and annoyed at him for mocking that fool Myth of Er. If he could calm her down, talk sense to her, she'd see what a strong voice of reason he would be as a mate.

It didn't matter if she loved him or even liked him. But their lives would go more smoothly if she at least respected him. And they would have a life together. Of that, he was certain.

He was a good deal behind her when he saw her dart into the woods. Hurrying his pace so he wouldn't lose her, he caught up and spied the light color of her dress moving through the trees.

Creeping silently, he hid behind a tree to observe the other figure that had appeared. She was speaking to someone.

Who?

Artem? The dirty vagrant?

Before Macar's disbelieving eyes, Hyacinth threw her arms around Artem and they kissed.

From her balcony, Hyacinth looked out on the playing field as thunder blasted the sky. It was an ill omen. At the horizon, the Aegean was blanketed by black clouds. The storm was still out at sea but the sky above them was gray, and the foul weather appeared to be rolling ever closer to land.

Her eyes were not on the competitors who were lined up for the javelin competition. Instead, she scanned the crowd that had come to watch, searching for Artem. Like Odysseus who had returned from the Long War to save Penelope from the greedy suitors who only loved her wealth, perhaps Artem would show up, shedding a disguise at the last moment. Just as Odysseus had used his expertise with a bow to best the others, Artem might step forward and win her.

This could yet happen. At the moment, though, Artem was nowhere to be seen.

Still, he had promised her he would be there.

Macar was highly visible, so clearly the champion. He'd already won the long jump and the wrestling competitions.

The archery event arrived with no sign of Artem. When the event ended, Macar was again the winner. The skies opened, releasing torrents of rain.

Hyacinth rushed to her bedchamber, her eyes as wet as the ground. Why had Artem not come? Had he no desire for the comforts of the life she could give him? Had he no desire for her?

Throwing herself onto her bed, she sobbed. Lightning flashed with angry illumination. She was glad of the weather. It suited her mood.

In about a half an hour, her mother came in. She spoke gently though her words were firm. "You dishonor Macar by not congratulating him. Arise and go to your future husband, Hyacinth."

Hyacinth looked up, pushing back her tear-soaked hair. Before she could protest, her father flew into the doorway.

He leaned in the entrance, red-faced and breathing heavily. "I have received the worst news just now!" he announced, and he was so overwrought that Hyacinth feared he would collapse there on the floor.

"What?" her mother asked, bolstering her husband at his side.

"A lone messenger has rowed ashore with the news. My ships have sunk in the storm. Our fortune is gone!" he wailed.

"All praise to Poseidon!" Hyacinth whispered, suddenly filled with new hope.

She rushed past her parents in the doorway and ran at top speed down into the yard. The rain soaked her in an instant but she didn't care. She had to find Artem.

Her dowry wasn't important to him. He would have her as she was. They could go away together. Their life would be rich with adventure. Others might think her crazy but she knew this was not true. Being with Artem was the only thing that had ever made sense to her.

Leaves spilled water on her as she crashed through the branches of the woods, running toward Artem's campsite.

A ring of sodden ashes was the only thing that remained of it.

Maybe she could find him at the shore.

Dashing through the woods, she came out to the shoreline. Rain pelted the ocean water. A gray cloud sat on the land.

He was gone.

Gone.

It had been over two weeks since the competition and Artem still lay on a cot in a small room behind the fish stall. Nadim the fish man came in. "How do you feel?" he asked.

"Grateful for your kindness," Artem replied.

Nadim grunted. "I still say we should call for Macar's arrest. A man should not be free to beat another man nearly to death and get away with it. What if I had not found you lying there senseless? You would be dead now!"

"We were both trespassing and poaching another man's land. Macar would say that he was defending his friend and host. We would benefit nothing from making such a charge and lay ourselves open to be arrested in return. Besides, I am on the mend and you will soon be free of me."

"Will you go to find the girl, the one for whom you cried out every night in your delirium?" Nadim asked.

Artem shook his head. "She must be married by now. Besides, I am sure she loathes me. I broke my promise to compete for her."

"You were hardly in any shape to compete, let alone walk," Nadim reminded him. "I have heard news of this girl. I inquired of Charis, the slave with whom she comes to market. She has not married. Her dowry lies at the bottom of the sea."

Artem sat upright excitedly. "You are a true friend to bring such welcome news! Can you send a message to her through Charis? Say I will come to her as soon as I can move on my own legs. Tell her I will enter the Olympic competition and use the prize to take her away with me."

Nadim took a pouch from his belt and opened its contents onto his outstretched palm. "These might advance your cause," he said. He held out two large, dark green, pear-shaped drop earrings.

"They're spectacular," Artem remarked. "But I cannot take them from you."

"They're yours," Nadim informed him. "I knew Herata, the old slave woman who found you. These were in an envelope along with the note pinned to your blanket. She was afraid someone would steal them from her so she asked me to hold on to them for when you were older. I believe the gem is called an evening emerald because it shines even more brightly in the lamplight. The time has come for me to turn them over."

Awestruck by the magnificence of the jewels, Artem was filled with resolve. "Tell her," he urged Nadim. "Tell her to hold on. I am coming for her."

Hyacinth caressed the emerging clay form as it spun on the potter's wheel. The soon-to-be urn that she rounded and lengthened on the wheel was turning out well. Life as a priestess of Athena had opened up so many new worlds to her. Her days were spent attending to the high priestess and learning so many things.

She had learned to create pottery, as she'd always wanted to. As she'd long suspected, she possessed a natural aptitude for it, taking to the craft with a sure, almost practiced hand.

It didn't blot out the dull sadness that had lived in her heart since the day Artem had disappeared, but it was satisfying nonetheless. And it was better than spending her days as Macar's pampered but servile wife.

Stopping the wheel, she surveyed her work. The result pleased her.

She was proud to serve Athena. She'd learned that the goddess was the patron of weavers, potters, goldsmiths, sculptors, musicians, and horsemen. As a priestess of Athena, and an accomplished potter as well, she had some status. Though she was forbidden to leave the grand, pillared temple on the Acropolis, in many ways she had become her own woman.

After setting the pot into the kiln, she washed her hands and prepared to go rinse off the rest of the clay. She was fairly covered in it, with it on her clothing, face, and even in her hair.

To get to her chamber, she had to cross the great, two-story central hall of Athena with its towering statue of the goddess. She stopped, as she always did, to look up and mar-vel at the majesty and power of Athena. Openings in the roof let slats of sunlight into the shadowy hall. They illu-minated the huge statue, imbuing it with a lifelike quality.

In one uplifted hand, Athena held the winged Nike, the goddess of victory. In her other, she wielded a spear. At her feet were a snake and a wheel. The tall, golden, spiked crown on her head dazzled in the sun.

Athena, goddess of, among much else, knowledge: More than anything that this life had brought to Hyacinth, she most valued that in the last few months she had begun to read. After Artem had disappeared, she'd despaired of ever learning. But now, like a miracle, under the tutelage of older priestesses, she had mastered the art. He had been right; it was as though a thousand locked doors had been suddenly flung open for her.

What a gift! Such richness!

Her reading was still rudimentary, but the other priest-esses could read skillfully. They read to one another, all variety of things. In the last weeks, she had learned about the medicines of Hippocrates, the thoughts of Socrates and Plato, the plays of Aristophanes. It was more knowledge than she could have ever imagined would come to her.

A priestess in a simple, belted, pale yellow dress came into the room so silently that Hyacinth started when she touched her arm. It was Iphigenia, a servant of the high priestess. Her green eyes flashed and she tossed back red curls as she delivered her message. "A young man wishes to speak to you. He is not allowed in the temple so I have made him wait outside."

Hyacinth looked at her sharply. "Do you know his name?"

"His name is Artem."

Artem — after all this time.

A vision of him appeared in her mind's eye.

"Remember that you are sworn to Athena now," Iphigenia reminded her.

Hyacinth bit her lip. Her eyes traveled up to Athena, the goddess who had provided this new life. Macar had not wanted her after her dowry was lost. Artem had not even appeared. But Athena had been here waiting to take her in.

"Please tell him to go," she said to Iphigenia. With a small nod of consent, Iphigenia departed.

Hyacinth's stomach clenched with anguish. Had this been the right choice? She should have at least spoken to him.

But if she saw him, she'd be swayed. And she could not run away with him now. To leave would be to disgrace not only herself but her whole family, and their lives had become difficult enough with their newly reduced circumstances.

Her position as a priestess was the only thing of social status they had left.

But Artem had come for her.

Filled with conflicting, confused feelings, she hurried from the Great Hall and up to her chamber. It was a small room with only a bowl and a water pitcher on a nightstand beside a bed. It had a narrow balcony, though, from which she could gaze down the steep slope of the Acropolis. Her balcony door was open now, and warm breezes blew into her room.

Sitting on her bed, she let her head drop into her hand. Her orange and black cat, Baby, leaped lightly onto the bed and licked her arm consolingly.

"Artem," she said softly, just for the pleasure of hearing his name. Lifting the cat onto her lap, she stroked its fur. "Artem," she whispered again.

A quick bang from the balcony made her jump.

The small blue violet plant she had placed on the railing had fallen down — blown by the breeze, no doubt. She was stepping out onto the balcony to right it when a hand touched her shoulder.

Gasping, she pulled away.

"I had to see you," Artem said. "Why did you not wait for me?"

"Wait for you?"

"I sent word with Charis, your slave woman."

She shook her head, not understanding. "I received no message."

He told her all that had happened. Hyacinth cursed Macar for the pain he'd caused them both. "And Charis, too. No doubt she received the message but didn't see fit to pass it along to me," she said.

"Only now have I recovered enough to come to you," he explained.

"If only I'd known," she said, dropping her head. A tear wound its way down the planes of her face and she didn't bother to wipe it away. "Now it's too late."

"It can't be," he protested fiercely. "The gods would not play with us so."

She laughed bitterly as a torrent of tears soaked her cheeks. "We are only playthings to the gods," she said, her voice cracked with sorrow. "They must be very entertained indeed at this turn of events." Breaking down completely, she buried her face in her hands and sobbed.

"No," he insisted. "If this is the will of the gods, then I defy them. I do not agree to be blown by the winds of some divine game." Turning his face up to the sky, he hissed in an intense whisper, "Hear me, gods of Olympus! I do not submit to your will. Curse me as you choose but I do not care — my destiny is my own and I will have this woman whom you have so laughingly taken from my side."

Hyacinth clutched his arm. "Do not tempt fate. The gods are powerful. They hear your defiant words and will destroy you."

Artem laid the tip of his fingers gently over her lips to stop her fearful rush of words. He shook his head as he wiped the tears from her face with his other hand. "Athena does not want your service if your heart is elsewhere. I'll win the Olympic archery contest — there is no one better with a bow and arrow — and we will go away together with the prize money."

He was so sure. If only she could feel as confident.

Artem reached for her hand and poured the contents of a pouch into her palm.

She drew in a sharp breath.

The green earrings sparkled in the sun.

"They are beautiful," she said, struck with awe. She looked at him with sudden alarm. "Where did you get them?"

"I didn't steal them, if that's what worries you," he said with a note of bitter chagrin at her assumption. "It seems they are my inheritance, all I have of value — and I give them to you."

"I would so love to have them, Artem. They are amazing of themselves and as a token of your love, even more so."

"They're yours to keep."

Tears began anew, streaming down her cheeks, spattering the air as she shook her downcast head. "My family would be in disgrace. Their lives would be completely destroyed."

"What of my life?" he countered. "It is over if I don't have you."

"Your life will go on. It must. You will meet another. You will be happy yet. My family cannot recover as you will be able to. You must go. Take back these gorgeous earrings and please leave."

He pressed the earrings into her hand. "Is it what you really want me to do?"

Bitter, salt tears fell on the green stones in her hands. "No! You know it's not what I want, but you have to go," she insisted. "Please go," she whispered, her voice barely audible.

He swung his legs over the balcony and prepared to climb down. "Keep the earrings," he said. "If the gods can't stop me, neither can your sense of duty. I refuse to give up on our love, Hyacinth. It comes from a place older and more sacred than even the gods themselves know of."

His words struck her as true and yet dangerously irreverent. "There is no place older and more sacred than Olympus," she said.

"There is, and it is in us," he insisted.

She held the earrings out to him. "You must take these. Give them to another who is free to accept your love."

Artem wrapped Hyacinth's fingers around the green gems and squeezed her hand. "There is no one else I will love."

He swung his legs over the balcony and prepared to climb down. "Keep these," he said. "Give them back to me on the day when you are sure you do not love me."

Artem sat on the Acropolis playing his flute. Months had passed since he last saw Hyacinth. As he had predicted, he had won the Olympic gold medal at the archery competition. He'd even had the pleasure of beating Macar. He didn't know which had been sweeter, winning the prize or seeing that fool's face twisted in outrage when he saw who had beaten him.

But still, Hyacinth would not see him. Each time he came to the temple of Athena, she sent the shifty-eyed Iphigenia to send him away.

He was not so easily deterred. Night after night, he sat under her balcony playing his flute. He would break and recite his poem of ancient Egypt which he had completed during his long recuperation from Macar's beating.

It was no longer just a story of a Nubian slave captive in Egypt. Now it told of an Egyptian woman he had loved. They had escaped from Egypt together and sailed south down the Nile. The song was rich with images of the golden sands, the imposing pyramids, and then the majestic temples and palaces of Nubia, the slave's beloved home.

These pictures had come to him in a rush of inspiration

sent, he had no doubt, from the muses of Mount Olympus, the divine creatures who inspired all the arts. Where else imaginings like that could originate in one such as himself who had never been out of Athens, he could not think.

And then one night, she appeared. How his heart had leaped at the sight of her, the silken dark hair, her form so desirable silhouetted there in the lamplight. Standing on the balcony, she sang to the sound of his flute, singing the words of his poem that she had committed to memory. That voice! Surely the siren mermaids upon their rocky cliffs that had mesmerized countless sailors with their sorceress songs could not sing more beautifully than did Hyacinth.

In the light of the lamp hanging above her door, there shone a glint of brilliant green at the side of her chin. She wore his earrings! She loved him still!

But when he began to climb to her balcony, she turned and went inside, shutting the door behind her.

Curse her stubbornness — her foolish, misguided sense of duty! What had her family ever done for her but make her feel stupid and unworthy? It was her destiny to be with *him*! Why did she let fear and duty rule her in this way?

But even as he cursed her, his heart exploded with love for his beautiful girl, his Hyacinth. He would never give up on her.

Iphigenia stood in the doorway to Hyacinth's chamber. It was the feast of Pallas Athena, the one day of the year when they would go out among the people in celebration of Athena, the guardian of their city.

Hyacinth stood at the window, gazing out over the Acropolis. Her hair was done up in golden cords. Her tunic was a fresh one. She was absently humming a song that Iphigenia recognized. It was the song she sang at night to the one who had once been known as the wild boy.

Iphigenia's eyes roamed to the gorgeous green earrings, clasped one to the other and sitting in a ceramic dish on Hyacinth's night table. They were a gift from the wild boy — stolen by him, no doubt. Hyacinth never wore them in the temple. It had to be that she only wore them at night when the two of them made music together.

Nightly, Iphigenia had fallen asleep restlessly listening to that maddening song drifting into her room.

Hyacinth played such games with that poor fellow, singing to him and yet shutting her door on him, refusing to see him. Either she loved him or she didn't! Why did he put up with it?

And that stupid boy did not even recognize Iphigenia when he saw her. He had never noticed her, even before, when he had come by the temple begging for food. She was raised there, an orphan abandoned at the temple steps, raised by the priestesses. She had been sent out to bring the beggars food, he among them. He had never even looked at her.

But she had noticed him. If he had been singing under

her window, desiring *her* love — she would have been long gone from the temple.

How she hated Hyacinth. What foolish arrogance, to throw away that kind of adoration, a love Iphigenia would have given anything to possess.

Hyacinth noticed Iphigenia and turned away from her daydreams at the window. "Is it time to go?" she asked.

"Yes, the high priestess is ready. I've come to get you. Will you be wearing your lovely green earrings to the celebration?"

Hyacinth shook her head as she passed Iphigenia in the doorway. "Are you coming?"

"In a minute." Iphigenia waited until Hyacinth had gone down the steps to the Great Hall. Then she scooped the earrings out of the dish.

If she could not have the wild boy's love, then she would have his token.

Pressing the earrings to her lips in a breathless, greedy kiss, she hurried away to hide them in her chamber.

The parade to honor Athena had its finish back at the wide steps of the temple. Hyacinth stood behind the high priestess. A statue of Athena had been paraded through the streets. It was a third the size of the one in the Great Hall, but imposing just the same.

A sea of people had gathered in front of the temple.

The head of the Athenian government stepped forward. "To honor Athena," he proclaimed, "we present the winners of this year's Olympic Games."

Macar stepped forward, his medals around his neck, head high, eyes steely, self-impressed as ever. His gaze shot up to Hyacinth on the steps. For a second their eyes met before Macar looked away. No doubt he was ashamed at having refused to marry her after her dowry was lost at sea. Naturally, no one blamed him.

Hyacinth shivered, recalling what a narrow escape she'd had. Marriage to Macar would have been a loveless, dull conformity. Life as a priestess was infinitely better. She heard he'd married and was expecting a child. His new wife was probably perfectly happy to have such a prize for a husband. Hyacinth hoped so, anyway.

Two other medal-wearing young men followed Macar. And then came Artem, his medal in hand.

He looked at nothing but Hyacinth. His direct gaze caused her to look away with embarrassment, certain that everyone could see how he focused on her.

Yet it seemed that only Iphigenia was aware of it. She sent Hyacinth a darting glance which Hyacinth dared not acknowledge.

Each winner was asked to address the crowd. When it was Artem's turn, he spoke to the high priestess. "I would offer to Athena this Olympic gold medal and all its worth in the hope that I might claim your priestess Hyacinth as my bride."

The crowd gasped at the boldness of his declaration.

"I make this plea," Artem continued, "for I know she loves me but will not be mine because she would not disgrace the goddess by breaking her oath. Yet I would rather end my days now than live without her in my life."

The high priestess stepped forward to reply. "Your plea is touching, young man, but Hyacinth has sworn a pledge as binding as any marriage oath. I cannot accept your medal nor release her to you."

Turning back toward the temple, she bid Hyacinth and the other priestesses to follow her in. As she was about to enter, Hyacinth cast a glance over her shoulder. Artem stood with his eyes boring into her.

For the first time that afternoon, the temple of Athena seemed to Hyacinth like a living tomb. Kneeling before the immense statue, she prayed to the goddess for strength and self-discipline. To go away with Artem would be to invite ruin not only for herself but for her family. Oh, but the urge to do it was overpowering, especially after today.

She was so deep in thought that she didn't realize another person had come into the room and now stood beside her. But soon she became aware of the heat and energy of that presence. Opening her eyes, she stared up at an aged woman. Her long, wild, wiry white hair played around her face and shoulders. Her milky blue eyes were unfocused as she faced Hyacinth without speaking.

Hyacinth had never seen this blind woman before, but she knew who she was by reputation and descriptions from the other priestesses.

"You are the Oracle of Delphi," Hyacinth acknowledged in an awed whisper.

The Oracle was the great prophetess who foretold the future in words so difficult to decipher that only the learned could tease the meanings from what she said. Hyacinth assumed she had come to the temple because of the feast. Why, though, was she speaking to her now?

"You know me, for we have met before," the woman's voice rumbled, emanating richly from deep within her throat.

"No, surely not," Hyacinth dared to contradict her. "Perhaps you think I am someone else. I am Hyacinth of Athens, a new priestess of Athena."

"I know you," the Oracle said again, her voice rising in irritation.

Hyacinth cowered, scared that she had angered this powerful personage.

The Oracle lifted her arms, her wide sleeves draping. "You have been in the cave. I spied on you in the kitchen. I will bring you to fiery ruin. The jewel is not what you think. You must seek its meaning. If you seek me I will help you," she ranted.

Hyacinth strained to make sense of this. She had never been in a cave. She had sometimes been in a kitchen. At the mention of the jewel, she thought of her earrings.

"The one who comes for you with the jewel is your destiny."

Hyacinth gasped. Artem!

"The jewel will come between the two of you eternally if your heart is not pure."

"Please," Hyacinth said. "I don't understand."

"The unraveling is the journey," the Oracle replied.

Why wouldn't this woman speak plainly?! And why was she even speaking to her, someone of so little importance?

"My words will become plain in time," the Oracle continued, apparently reading Hyacinth's thoughts. "I come to you to pay a debt. I have wronged you before. The fates have commanded me to amend all I have wronged so that my powers might expand for the good of all."

"Tell me. Please. Should I go off with the one I love, the one who has given me the green jewels?" Hyacinth asked.

"The unraveling is the journey," the Oracle of Delphi said once more. Abruptly, she turned and, navigating her way with fluid grace, left the Great Hall.

That night, the rest of Athens reveled and celebrated the holiday. Lamplight and bonfires lit the black sky. On the Acropolis, though, low-lying clouds obliterated the moon's rays.

Iphigenia sat on her bed examining the stolen green earrings by the light of her small lantern. How they gleamed! Such elegance!

What a declaration he had made! And that idiot, that stupid girl, had stood there mute. *I would have run into his arms, forsaken everything for him.* Iphigenia was certain.

And then there it was — that flute playing once again out on the hill.

He was back! Would he return every night for all eternity?

It was maddening!

Still clutching the earrings, she stepped out onto the pitch darkness of her balcony to watch them as she'd often done before.

The flute playing stopped.

Hyacinth's balcony was dark, empty.

She had failed to come out. Would he finally give up?

Iphigenia's mind raced. Perhaps she should go down, make her feelings for him known, and tell him he could even call her Hyacinth if he wished. She wouldn't care — anything to have his love, to be taken away from this awful temple that had been her prison since childhood.

In the darkness, Iphigenia suddenly caught a sharp breath. An even blacker form was climbing over Hyacinth's balcony, climbing down.

She was going to him!

Iphigenia stood no chance with him now. "A curse on

you!" she spat as she hurled the green earrings over her balcony.

Hyacinth's foot ached as she searched for a foothold in the column below her balcony. It was so dark! Where was Selene, goddess of the moon, tonight when she needed her?

Why had he stopped playing the flute?

It was so dark. She prayed he hadn't gone. But perhaps she had no right to pray, now that she had broken her vow to Athena. Would she be cursed by the goddess for this?

Would Artem curse her as well? She was coming to him without the earrings that represented his love. Just a moment ago, she'd heard his flute and she'd decided that she could not go on living without him, that no price was too high to pay. She'd gone to put on the earrings, preparing to leave with him, only to discover that they were missing!

A quick, frantic search had not produced them.

They were utterly gone.

And then the music had stopped. Rushing to the balcony, she searched the darkness but could not see him. She could not let him leave, maybe forever.

That was when she had begun the climb down, too frantic to catch up to him to let worry about the earrings interfere. She was not sure how she would manage, but he had climbed up before . . . which meant she could climb down.

She was two body lengths from the bottom when the clouds parted and hit the landscape with moonlight.

With the brilliance of a shooting star, the green earrings flew through the air, sparkling in the white radiance of the moon.

It was a blessing from Athena! A sign that the goddess bore her no malice!

But what if Artem was down there, waiting hidden behind a tree or in a bush? What if he thought she had tossed the earrings down as a sign that she no longer loved him?

"Artem!" she called in a soft whisper, afraid to alert the other priestesses. "Artem!"

No answer came.

She saw the earrings glisten, caught in the nettles of a juniper bush at the edge of a rocky outcropping.

Then she detected him moving below in the places not touched by moonlight. He was going toward the earrings to retrieve them.

Still afraid to cry out to him, she judged that she could jump to the ground. She landed on her knees and her foot throbbed where it had banged on the dirt.

He had not reached the earrings yet. She had to get there first, be waiting for him with them glistening in her ears.

She was nearly there, reaching forward, balanced precariously over the rough juniper bush. In her rush to retrieve the earrings, she did not see him, also hurrying in the darkness.

He came upon her suddenly, unexpectedly, skidding to a stop.

Surprised, she stumbled back.

Her weak foot buckled and caved under her weight. Suddenly she was pitching forward uncontrollably, tumbling down the hillside.

Tumbling, bouncing, hitting and hitting again.

She heard something snap.

Then

My Artem, I am so sorry. You have no idea how it pains me to see you sob. How I hoped that at last we could be together. How I wanted to sail away, maybe to your golden Egypt, where no one could find us.

You do not hear me, so deep is your grief.

You throw your body on top of mine as you howl at the moon like a mad wolf.

I am not there anymore.

I am no longer the young woman whose hair has come unbound and trails to the ground as he carries her broken body up the steep hill to the temple of Athena.

He and Iphigenia bring her inside. The high priestess comes and cries out in alarm.

Still weeping, Artem leaves. I call out to him but he does not turn back to me.

No one speaks to me at all. Silently I watch as my dead body is washed, dressed in a new tunic, and laid in a coffin. Ashes are scattered in her loose hair. A wreath of hyacinths is placed on her head.

Hyacinths.

I think this word has a meaning to me but I am

forgetting. I can't remember my name, nor my mother or father.

Trying to remember these things, I wander down the sloping Acropolis and through the streets of Athens. It is not safe for a young woman to walk through silent Athens in the night. I know this and yet I am strangely unafraid.

I turn down an unfamiliar city street, and at the end of it I come to a river. A flat boat floats, moored to a post jutting from the water. On it, a man in a rough, brown toga stands as though he is waiting for me.

This must be a dream, I think, despite the fact that it seems so real.

"I will ferry you to the other side," the man offers.

"What is on the other side?" I ask.

"You will like it," he says.

"I have no way to pay you."

"That gold cord ensnarled in your hair will do."

I pick through my knotted locks, freeing the remaining piece of broken cord. "It's not worth much," I mention.

"It's enough."

I dimly recall a tale Charis told me as a girl. The story does not return to me clearly, though I remember the moral. Don't pay the ferryman until he gets you safely to the other side, otherwise he will dump you in the middle of the River Styx.

"Is this the River Styx?" I ask.

He nods, and I shiver with fear. This is the river of death. On the other side is the underworld.

Fearfully, I crumple the golden cord in my fist. "No. No." I back away.

I buckle forward, sure I will vomit. I only dry heave, producing nothing. My eyes tingle with tears yet remain dry.

The ferryman beckons for me to come. "You will regret life as a spirit," he says. "Such unimaginable loneliness. This is your one chance to cross over."

"I will pay you on the other side," I offer.

He smiles bitterly, shaking his head. "Now they tell even young people that story, I see. Sad to make the young so untrusting. Pay me when you wish."

As I step into the boat, he unties and pushes off with his pole. The silent black river flows past the home of my parents and brothers. A jar of hyssop water sits at the front door to show there has been a death in the family.

The river flows along the coast where Artem sits on a rock, the ocean waves crashing around him. "Don't!" I cry as he hurls the hooked-together earrings into the waves.

"Good-bye. Good-bye," I call to him. He looks up for a moment as though he might have heard me on the wind or in the surf. Then he hangs his head in despair.

It is dawn by the time the boat reaches the other

side. As it bumps onto the shore, I hand the ferryman his golden cord. Then he is gone, nowhere to be seen.

I am soon in a meadow with others. It's full of flowers with a warm breeze wafting through. We talk and rest. I am aware of being very tired.

Time ceases to be meaningful. I might have been in the meadow for hundreds of years, maybe hundreds of minutes.

It is all the same to me.

There seems to be a great deal to think about, to sort out, make some sense of. We are always talking to one another, discussing, wondering if we made the best choices while we lived:

"What do you think I should have done differently?"

"What would you have done if you had been me?"

"Was I wrong to put aside love for a higher good?"

"Is it so wrong to want to be safe?"

"Did I do that for the right reasons?"

It went on and on . . . and on.

We are never hungry but we drink as though parched from the two rivers than run through the meadow, Lethe and Amelete. I notice that the more I drink, the less I can remember of the past.

Each time I drink from the river, I sleep a good deal. After one very long, deep slumber, I awake in the meadow and think: *I would like to try again.*

Then, soon after I have this thought, a column of blinding white light appears. It has a name that I have heard from the others in the meadow.

It is The Hinge of the Universe.

It hums steadily, vibrating at a very fast rate.

I have seen it before and watched others walk into its light, but it has never before affected me. Now this day, I am unable to resist its pull; I want to go toward it.

I am in its center.

In a rapid stream, I am shooting downward, through a starstruck black expanse, toward the earth.

I am returning.

I will be done with the world that makes me hang on the whims of men. I will make my own power. I will serve the mother goddess and draw strength from her.

(On the Wheel of Rebirth)

Canaan, 28 C.E.:

My dear brother, Thaddeus,

It was a fine wedding even though the host ran out of wine at one point. It seems that this Jesus of Nazareth that they're all talking about produced lots more of it somehow after his mother requested that he do so — a man after my own heart.

I've got to stop drinking so much wine. It makes these headaches of mine even worse. I also become too quarrelsome when I drink. For example, some folks were claiming that this Jesus I mentioned is the messiah that has been prophesied. I quickly argued that this could not be. According to prophesy, the messiah isn't supposed to come until *after* the prophet Elijah returns from the dead.

So there. I had them on that.

I didn't even know that this Jesus had been listening, but he had. He said: *I say to you that Elijah has come already and they did not know him.*

I told him: "Well, okay. If you say so." But to be honest, this mystified me so I asked around about what he meant by that. The group of twelve men who travel with him told me that they're fairly convinced that he means that Elijah *was* born again, this time as John the Baptist. Then, when he had his head cut off, it was more of that karma stuff we heard about from the Buddha texts. It seems Elijah was responsible for having some heads chopped off way back when. So it came back to him in his next life.

Elijah reincarnated as John the Baptist and that means it was all clear for the messiah to come. I can accept that. Reincarnation is certainly not a new idea.

Okay, I say. Fair enough.

I'm definitely going to stop drinking so much, though.

London, England, 1247:

My darling baby Gwendolyn, I give you to these good nuns of the Order of the Star of Bethlehem since I am too poor to feed you on my own. Hopefully they will raise you to be a pious nun and to serve God, especially Mary, the mother of God, as they do. Your life will be plain and holy but you will never starve. You will not have to concern yourself with life's difficult choices.

It is a good time in England. Edward the First is a good king. Stay true to God and country and you will never go wrong.

London, England, 1348:

Rest in Peace, Mother Abbess Maria Regina (born Gwendolyn of Canterbury), leader of our order who has this day died of the terrible Black Death that has taken so many others. Your devotion to Mary, our divine mother, knows no equal. Your tender ministrations to the sick and dying will not soon be forgotten. Your prodigious knowledge of Latin and Greek unlocked a world of learning to the sisters of our order.

Captain's log, 1518:

We arrived on the coast of West Africa today where we dropped anchor offshore for fear of being attacked or contracting any of the native diseases that so many before us have succumbed to. My jaw is aching. No doubt I have begun to grind my teeth at night once again due to the pressures of this arduous journey and the long, steamy nights. I pray it is not lockjaw, as I did cut myself on a rusted nail earlier in the week.

Finally, after three days at anchor, representatives of one of the coastal tribes trading in slaves rowed out to us in a long boat loaded with men, women, and children. The head man informed me that these bound captives were from a neighboring, inland tribe that were captured during a raid.

There was much wailing and crying out, especially from mother to child and vice versa, as we loaded them below the decks of our ship, lying them down side by side in order to fit as much cargo as possible. We paid for them with rum, trinkets, and some swords.

As a gesture of good faith, the head trader of the coastal tribe made me a gift of a finely carved spear, since, on our last visit, I made known to him that I am a collector of javelins, lances, and spears. I assured him I was most appreciative of it and would return in six months' time for additional cargo.

My first mate, an experienced sailor who was undertaking his very first voyage on a slave ship, had heretofore proven to be a skilled and able-bodied seaman. Upon seeing the slaves shackled in iron at hand and foot, he claimed to be sickened by our endeavor, saying that he had not realized it would affect him as profoundly as it did. He proved this almost immediately by vomiting copiously over the side of the ship. Then he claimed that violent headaches he'd suffered as a boy had returned, reactivated by his monstrous guilt. They were of such force that he felt overwhelmed and unable to perform his duties. He asked to be allowed to go ashore and quit my service.

I replied that once we have anchored at the Caribbean island of Hispaniola, where we will dispatch the captives to the slave trader who has contracted this expedition, he was free to leave my employ. Until such time he was duty bound to honor the terms of his employment, however repugnant he found them. Otherwise I would not think twice about tossing him overboard into the shark-infested waters.

I will long remember the hatred in his eyes as he lowered

his head and bowed in compliance. It was with some relief that I watched him back away since, for the briefest moment, I envisioned him pulling his arm back and releasing a staggering blow to my jaw. The image was incredibly vivid and I am glad to say it did not occur.

I will lock my cabin this night, so intense was the loathing I sensed he bore me. I regretted having to speak to him so harshly, but it is incumbent upon me as captain of this ship to maintain order. If I do not keep control, uprising and mutiny will follow.

Expedition to the New World under Francisco Pizarro, 6 June 1532:

Today I must make a sad entry in my journal, this record of the wondrous things my eyes have beheld in this moist, lush, gold-drenched new world.

For many years before joining this expedition, I sailed wherever I could find work as seaman. As a young man I even made it as far as the coasts of western Africa, though those memories I would rather forget. The Spanish fleets on which I have sailed of late are the finest in the world, and I have seen much of it in my wide-flung travels. I must say with all sincerity that the wonders of this strange new world with its exotic foliage, its temples and carvings, its abundance of gold and jewels, defy my very imagination. The leader of the native people, the

Incas, wears a crown beset with hundreds of emeralds. This astounding jewel is mined in abundance in this land, although the leaders of the people refuse to reveal the pathways into the mines to Pizarro.

I write today with sorrow, as I mentioned before. One of the most remarkable women I have ever met has passed away. I must record the passing of the Priestess Acana since her people, the mighty Incas, though possessing a high culture, have not the gift of writing and cannot record her life story.

Acana was the keeper of the sacred emerald of her people, which they called Mother of Emeralds and worshipped devotedly. Her position was one of great respect. She spent her days fashioning exquisite vessels to be used in sacred ceremonies and singing as she configured astrological charts. This holy woman was in possession of a voice that could hypnotize. Often she could be seen walking through the jungle, her pet jaguar strolling tamely by her side.

Acana has today succumbed to a disease I fear has come from our party of explorers. At the end of her days she labored mightily to save her people who have been dying of the pox in great numbers. What cruelty that she who had learned the ancient medicines of her people, who developed new treatments from barks and roots, could do nothing to cure her own ills.

I have been to the courts of Spain and spoken to the wisest men in Europe but never have I met a person of such learning as Acana.

From the diary of Abigail O'Brian, 1687:

I guess today is my lucky day. I could sure use one. Seems there has been no luck coming to me since I foolishly followed my fellow aboard a ship docked in the port of Dublin and bound for the colonies in North America. He said he adored my bright eyes and red curls and would be true to me for all my days. I suppose a man will say anything when he's drunk. More the fool was I to believe him.

The captain told the seventy or so of us onboard that the passage was free. All we need do is work for a master in America for six or seven years as something he called an indentured servant and it would be taken care of. We wouldn't be paid nothing for our work but we'd be housed and fed, so who needs money anyway?

It didn't occur to me that there was anything wrong with this deal until we were too far out to sea to do anything about it. We got little to eat, one lump of hard fresh bread every two weeks of the twelve-week journey. After five weeks one married couple begged to be thrown overboard then and there rather than endure another day of hunger. They were told to go back below where they did die of weakness and starvation before the journey's end. The dysentery was a nightmare down there; the stench was unbearable. By the sixth week my fellow had found himself a new girl, her husband having died of the pox and been thrown overboard two weeks earlier. I'd grown so fed up with him I can't say I was sorry to see him go.

I thought I was glad when the trip ended, but little did I know that my troubles were just beginning. We landed in Virginia where a man took all of us to work on his tobacco farm. You've never done backbreaking work until you've picked tobacco, though I hear those that pick cotton have it even worse. We had to work alongside slaves from Africa. Most of them could not even speak English but talked only to one another in the most foreign language I've ever heard.

I've been too bone tired to write in this diary but finally I got a break. The man in Virginia lost a third of his indentured servants in a poker game to a man named Wheldon living in a place called New England. As long as there are no tobacco fields, it's got to be better than where I am.

Mr. Charles Wheldon, Esq.
Salem, Massachusetts
March 3, 1691

Dear Mr. Wheldon,
This letter is to inform you that in a week's time I will be putting my daughter, Elizabeth May, on a boat heading for the town of Salem in the colonies. She is aware that, when last you were in England, you consulted me regarding your honorable intentions to wed her. She has assured me that, though the two of you are not well acquainted, she is favorably disposed toward what she does know of your appearance and disposition which

you made known to her on your several visits to our home with your esteemed father.

Elizabeth May has been well educated, having read the classics in my well-stocked library, the very one your esteemed father remarked upon so favorably when last we saw you. She has also been taught by a governess well-versed in Latin, history, and French. The life of the mind is of utmost interest to my daughter but I trust you will find her a lively enough companion as she has always been a girl of spirit. It will bode well for your happiness together if you could see your way to providing her with a supply of books as well as stimulating pursuits that will satisfy her active mind.

As you are aware, Elizabeth May has just this month attained her seventeenth birthday. My wife, Mrs. Harrington, and I are certain she is mature enough to make you a fine wife but I pray you will keep in mind her tender age while at the same time patiently guiding her with the benefit of your experience. I am confident you will treat her well since she will know no other in this new land into which she is to come. Were I not certain of your fine character, I would not send her so far from home.

Sincerely,
Mr. Henry Harrington
London, England

Salem, Massachusetts, 1691

Charles Wheldon clapped the snow from his gloves as he entered the front door. As usual, his young wife, Elizabeth May, was on the couch in the library reading. At his arrival, she looked up from her book.

"What brings you home so soon?" she asked.

"My court case was postponed."

"Why?" She put down her book and approached him.

He made an aggravated, dismissive grunt. "The Lewis sisters were in court. They claim to have seen witches flying through the air on poles and believe they recognized one of them to be their neighbor."

"Are they believed?" Elizabeth May bent down to pet her black cat, who had padded in from the library after her.

"Yes, by many," he told her. "Of late this town has gone mad with sightings of witches."

Elizabeth May's hand flew to her mouth as she gasped. Expressions like this reminded him of how young she was, despite her wifely position. "I hope the Lewis sisters are not pointing a finger at old Miss Pritchard."

He looked at her sharply. "Why should she be suspect?"

"She grew up on the island of Barbados and knows a great deal of the ancient folk cures of the place. Besides that, she's always talking of omens and what they might foretell."

"I would advise her to keep such notions to herself. The penalty for witchcraft is death."

"I will tell her," Elizabeth May agreed, heading for the winter bonnet and cape she kept hung on a peg by the front door.

Charles held up his hand. "On second thought, do not. We want no guilt by association."

"I'll tell her what is afoot and then leave," Elizabeth May replied.

"It's none of our business."

"But they hanged Jane Stewart as a witch just last month!" she protested.

"That woman should have been in an asylum," he reminded her. "She spit at every citizen who crossed her path, hurling vile curses at them."

"That did not make her a witch. She was more to be pitied than despised," Elizabeth May insisted.

"Her hanging was also a small loss. These witch hunts cull criminals, deviants, the indigent, and the insane from our society."

"That's harsh. Besides, Miss Pritchard is none of those, but she is a single lady who does not attend church and is therefore a target," Elizabeth May pressed.

"If she does not attend church, then she must take her chances."

"Charles! The woman is old and blind."

"I forbid it!" Charles insisted firmly. His tone was raised just enough to mean that this was his final word on the subject. "And perhaps that cat of yours should be gotten rid of. You know what they're saying about cats, I'm sure."

Elizabeth May scooped up her cat, cradling it in her arms. Lowering her eyes in that way she had, she bowed slightly before retreating back into the library. Those falsely humble lowered eyes infuriated him. He had seen indentured servants and slaves make the same compliant nod too many times not to understand the contempt it masked. *Yes, sir. Thank you, sir. I'll stab you in your sleep first chance I get, sir.*

It was not a look he desired to see in his wife. But then, he had come to see many things in his new wife that he wished were not there.

He hung his coat and hat in the front closet and went to his study. This delay in the court hearing had been a reprieve of sorts. The man he was defending, Mr. Woolcot, had sold another man, Mr. Matherson, a horse that turned out to be lame.

Mr. Woolcot claimed he had no knowledge of this infirmity and had made the deal in good faith. Was he required to take back the horse and return the money? Charles's client said no, but Mr. Matherson had disagreed and sued.

Taking down one of his law books from the shelf, Charles opened it in the hope of finding a legal precedent for such a situation. He had found several cases that were similar but searched for one that was exactly the same and would thus make this an easy and swift hearing.

With his mind drifting off the case at hand, he absently rubbed his jaw.

He noticed it was painful. Had he been grinding his teeth at night again? If so, it usually meant something was weighing on his mind. It was not the legal case at hand, though it was, in a way, related to it: Should Mr. Henry Harrington be expected to take back his daughter and reimburse Charles for her expenses? Just as with Mr. Matherson, what Charles had gotten was not what he had expected.

Though lovely to look at, Elizabeth May was stubborn, willful, nearly addicted to reading, and insatiably curious about everything besides her husband. When it came to him, Elizabeth May all but implied he was some sort of petty tyrant, duly bound to the status quo, and someone whose wishes and rules were simply to be gotten around by secrecy and deception. In short, she behaved as a child — granted, a smart and pretty child, but her mind was immature, nonetheless.

It was perhaps partly his fault for choosing such a young bride, barely seventeen, when he was nearly twenty-four. But he had been so taken with her when he first saw her in London. She conversed so intelligently on a number of subjects, including medicine and history. She even had knowledge of geology. When he had mentioned that he might invest in an emerald mine in Rhodesia, she had supplied the fact that polished emeralds came from beryl, a mineral found in aluminum beryllium silicate.

He'd been impressed. Who wouldn't be?

At the time she had struck him as the most desirable possible wife, a mate young enough to adapt herself to the harshness of life in the colonies and learned enough not to bore him to tears during the long, hard winters.

What, though, had impressed her about him?

Many women had desired to marry him. And why not? He was handsome, from a well-to-do family, and a lawyer. Athletic in his build, he had been a star athlete in college, excelling at track and field events. He was confident in his demeanor, a natural leader among men.

Perhaps the more pertinent question was: What had disillusioned her about him in the six months since they had been married? What had brought on the polite distance between them?

Shrugging off this concern, he returned to his law book. Certainly it was not his fault if she behaved childishly; looking at him disapprovingly when he was sharp with the servants, narrowing her eyes at him for shooing a beggar from the back door. Order had to be maintained in a household, and it was up to him to do it.

An hour later, he had found the legal precedent he'd been searching for, and left his study. In the hall, he met Abby, the indentured servant who was one of their maids. His father had won her indenture papers in a poker game along with many others. He had given two of them to Charles and Elizabeth May as a wedding gift.

Abby plumped the red curls bundled at the back of her head in a seductive manner before dipping into a quick curtsy. "Good evening, sir," she said, her voice warm and caressing.

"Tell Missus Wheldon I am ready for lunch," he requested.

"I'm afraid Missus Wheldon has gone out, sir."

"Out? Do you know where?"

"No, sir."

He rubbed his jaw. He was fairly certain he knew where she'd gone.

Elizabeth May lifted her long dress above the swirling snow drift as she rapped on the back door of Miss Pritchard's house. It was answered by Lily, the family slave Miss Pritchard had brought with her from Barbados. "Come in, child," Lily said in her thick island accent. "It is near to a blizzard out there." With vigorous slaps she brushed the snow from Elizabeth May's cloak. "Oh, I can never get used to this wretched climate. It's what will kill me in the end," she said. "Have you come for another herbal poultice wrap to soothe that ankle of yours? Is it bothering you again?"

"No. Thanks, Lily. Thanks to your good medicine my ankle has not bothered me of late. I've come to speak to Miss Pritchard about some news I believe is of importance to her," Elizabeth May revealed as she hung up her cloak and bonnet on the pegs near the wood-burning stove.

"The Missus will be up from her midday napping soon. Let me make you a cup of tea in the parlor, and you can wait for her there."

"I'd just as soon take it here with you," Elizabeth May said.

"If that pleases you," Lily agreed. "It's not the proper thing, but Miss Pritchard is not fussy about such as that."

Lily made the tea while Elizabeth May told her what she'd learned of the witchcraft accusations. Lily's cheerful expression melted into a scowl of concern. "No one has come to involve us with such a thing — not yet, anyway," she said as she put the tea kettle over the iron hot plate atop the burning stove.

Elizabeth May noticed several cats strolling through the kitchen. A gray tabby cat leaped up onto the table and Lily quickly shooed it off again. "How many cats have you got?" Elizabeth May asked.

"Oh, I've lost count," she replied. "Miss Pritchard is so good-hearted. She can never turn away a stray. More and more cats seem to be homeless these days. It's as if people don't want to be associated with them anymore."

Miss Pritchard appeared in the doorway. Her long white hair was loosely splayed over the shoulders of her black robe. Elizabeth May found the white-blue blankness of the woman's blind eyes unsettling, and made an effort not to stare at them.

"Miss Elizabeth has come to visit us," Lily informed Miss Pritchard. "She is here at the table."

"I am aware. Thank you, Lily." The old woman took a seat across from Elizabeth May. "This is a pleasant surprise. What brings you here, my girl?"

"Troubling news, I fear." She told her what she'd heard from Charles.

"And you naturally assumed I was the witch these girls saw riding across the sky, did you?" Miss Pritchard asked, an amused smile playing on her thin, lined lips.

Elizabeth May flushed with embarrassment. "I thought this only because you have been known to prescribe unusual cures for neighboring people."

"She learned it from my mama," Lily offered. "She was the cook for the Pritchards in Barbados."

"It's true," Miss Pritchard agreed. "Lily's mother taught me her island ways. When I was a girl, I believed everything she taught me. As I grew older, I came to realize that she believed many superstitious things that were not true. But she also knew many natural cures that worked."

"Mama taught you to heal by touch like she did," Lily reminded her.

"Life force, healing energy, runs through all living things," Miss Pritchard explained to Elizabeth May. "I have used my hands to direct this life force into a diseased or injured area."

"Do you believe in witches?" Elizabeth May asked.

"St. Augustine, a Catholic theologian of the ninth century, argued that only God can control the mechanisms of the universe. Neither the devil nor any human being has that same ability. That is what I believe."

"Are you a Catholic?" Elizabeth May asked.

"I do not believe in one religion or the other. I worship God privately and in my own way," Miss Pritchard replied. "God is God whatever you call him, or her."

Her? This idea hit Elizabeth May forcefully. "You think God could be a her?" she asked, leaning excitedly across the table. Despite all the teaching she'd received to the contrary, she'd always suspected God could be a female.

"Perhaps God is not he or she. Perhaps God is a force so vast it combines the sexes or disregards sex altogether," Miss Pritchard proposed.

God was *neither* male nor female? This was a new idea to Elizabeth May. She could not imagine a being or force beyond the confines of male or female. It gave her the feeling that her brain was being twisted, stretched in a manner that was almost painful. "I'll need to think further about that idea before I can rest easy with it," she admitted.

"Thinking deeply never killed anyone," said Miss Pritchard.

Lily laughed bitterly as she poured the tea for them. "I'm not so sure *that's* true," she commented.

After their tea, Elizabeth was full of questions regarding island cures. She and Lily followed Miss Pritchard into a small, disheveled study where Lily, under Miss Pritchard's direction, searched among books stacked in disarray. Despite the apparent chaos, she quickly found what she was looking for.

"These two books are the best ones I have," Miss Pritchard said. "Lily's mother gave them to me shortly before she passed away."

Elizabeth May took the books. Both were so frayed and faded with age that she worried that they might crumble to dust in her hands if she attempted to open either of them.

"You can borrow them for as long as you like," Miss Pritchard offered.

"Thank you. I should very much like to read them. It would be interesting to study medicine and become a doctor, though I realize no such opportunity is available to women."

Miss Pritchard sighed. "I know. It's so foolish and wrong. Women throughout history have been midwives and healers, delivering babies, caring for the sick. Why they should not be doctors is a mystery."

"It is no mystery," Lily disagreed. "It's because men won't let them. They want to keep all the power and knowledge for themselves."

"Lily," Miss Pritchard said. "Could you find me my special deck of tarot cards? I would like to do a reading for Elizabeth May."

Lily turned to Elizabeth May. "Miss Pritchard has special cuts in the cards that tell her which is which, even though she can't see them. There's no better card reader than Miss Pritchard. Even Mama said she was the best, although Mama herself taught her how to do it."

"I've never seen a tarot deck," Elizabeth May said.

Back at the kitchen table, Miss Pritchard spread the cards facedown with the assurance of a sighted person. She told Elizabeth May to select thirteen cards and leave them facedown, then she arranged them.

The first card she turned over was called The Lovers.

"This is your immediate past," Miss Pritchard said. "The card is upside down. You have lost a true love."

Elizabeth May gasped but said nothing. It was true, though she tried to push it from her mind and not dwell on the past.

Miss Pritchard stroked her hand consolingly. She turned the next card. "You will meet this love again," she said.

As she continued to turn cards, she revealed a tower being hit by lightning. "The tower card predicts a sudden upheaval, abrupt change."

"What will happen?" Elizabeth May asked.

"You will soon find out," said Miss Pritchard.

Abby stood at the bottom of the winding stairs and winced at the sounds of crashing as Mr. Wheldon threw things against the wall from upstairs. It was disconcerting how easily his temper flared. And no one got him angrier than that wife of his — a pretty young thing, to be sure, but with no sense whatsoever. Any other woman would consider herself lucky to have him, yet all she ever did was to resist his wishes at every turn. She'd try the patience of a saint — and he was far from saintly.

"Has she come back yet?" asked Helen, the kitchen maid, stepping out of the kitchen door.

Abby shook her head.

"I hope he calms down by the time she returns," Helen said.

"He told her not to go out but she went anyway. I don't know what she expected," Abby answered as another resounding crash hit.

Helen sighed anxiously and went back into the kitchen.

Abby gazed up the stairs. A man in a rage did not frighten her. In her day, she'd seen more than her share of them. She could handle him and maybe do herself some good in the process.

This latest upset had given her an idea. This wife of his would not last. The awful marriage would end sooner or later. Why shouldn't Abby nudge it along?

Abby knew men found her attractive. In Ireland or England it would be unheard of for a man such as Mr. Wheldon to think of marrying a maid — an indentured servant, at that. But her indenture was almost over and Americans were a practical people. A woman known to be a good housekeeper and pleasant, obedient company might make a swift and sensible replacement for a first wife who had deserted him — or who had been sent packing because she was thought to be unfaithful by her husband.

Of course, Abby did not know for certain that Elizabeth May had been unfaithful, but she had seen something that could serve as evidence that there was another man in her life. It might be enough to inflame an already agitated husband. Possibly, this was the perfect moment to show it to him.

Lifting her skirt daintily, she ascended the stairs.

Charles stood in the kitchen awaiting his wife's return, sure she would sneak in through the back door. He paced, agitated and ready to spring at her. It was nearly dark. What had she been doing all this time?

In the purple grayness of dusk, he caught sight of her trekking across their backyard in the falling snow, huddled into her cape. She saw him watching her at the back window. She stood stock still, and for a moment he thought she would run. He prepared himself to chase her, but after another second she continued toward the kitchen door.

"Where have you been?" he asked angrily as soon as she entered.

"I had to warn Miss Pritchard to be careful. I know she is no witch; she doesn't even believe in witches," Elizabeth May defended her actions.

"I do not know that you were even at Miss Pritchard's house. Maybe you are lying to me. Perhaps you have gone out to meet a lover. I have sent Abby over to Miss Pritchard's right now to check."

"What are you talking about?" she asked, astonished.

He had been certain she'd gone to warn the old blind woman and had been upstairs venting his rage. He was fed up with having such a defiant wife. It hadn't occurred to him that she was unfaithful to him until Abby had come in and shown him what she'd found.

Charles took a crisp, white handkerchief from his jacket pocket. He unfolded it, displaying what it held. Elizabeth May gasped when she saw what he had wrapped with the handkerchief.

"Where did you get those?" she asked.

A pair of dark green peridot earrings in the shape of teardrops lay hooked together in the center of the handkerchief. They glistened brilliantly.

She reached for the earrings but he yanked them back to his side. "I did not give them to you. I am sure of that."

"They were among my private possessions," she said. "You had no right to pry!"

"Abby thought they were from me to you. She came into our room to return them. She told me she'd found them on the floor and thought you'd dropped them. Thinking she was giving me a compliment, she said a loving look comes into your eye whenever you wear them. I have never seen you wear these. What man gave them to you?"

Elizabeth May seemed unable to speak, but stood there looking like she wanted to flee.

He was now sure she had a lover. It explained everything — her coldness to him, the fact that she had defied his instructions to go out in a snowstorm. And now he had the proof of her love affair in these earrings — a lavish gift, to be certain.

And that soft look in her eyes that Abby had described: There it was at this very instant.

"Tell me!" he shouted, slamming his hand on the table. "I demand to know!"

Elizabeth May sat at the maid's table in the kitchen. Under her snow-flecked cape, she clutched the books Miss Pritchard had lent her. To produce them now would simply fan the flames of his rage.

Brian. She remembered a pair of hazel green eyes set in a pale, handsome face; how his thick, nearly black hair settled in a wave across his forehead. She could hear his Irish brogue as he pressed the earrings into her hand: "There's a story to these earrings. My great-great-great-grandfather found them in the Irish Sea as he was swimming for his life. He was a Spanish sailor aboard the ship *Girona*, part of the Armada sent by Philip the Second of Spain to conquer England. His ship had been sunk by the English and he was swimming for shore as fast as he could when there in the water, no doubt stirred up from the bottom by the battle, these earrings floated right toward him. They were hooked together just as they are now."

Her father imported goods from Ireland and she had accompanied him to port one day. She had first laid eyes on Brian as he unloaded goods from the ship on which he'd worked as a sailor. The attraction between them had been instant. He lost no time in sitting down beside her on a bench while her father conducted his business elsewhere.

From then on, she accompanied her father to the port whenever she could. Brian sometimes came to London and found his way to her bedroom window. They would sit out on the porch roof until the morning. It was on a night such as that when he gave her the earrings. "I want you to have them," he'd said. Minutes after he'd spoken those words, the window to her bedroom was flung open and her father stepped onto the roof, firearm in his hands. Without asking a question, he'd shot just slightly over Brian's head.

Elizabeth May had screamed as, terrified, he'd slid from the roof, crashing into the bushes below. "If you ever come near my daughter again I'll blow your head off!" Henry Harrington shouted after him.

Shaking, Elizabeth May had slipped the earrings into the pocket of her skirt just before he whirled around on her, red-faced with anger. "Get inside, you shameless girl. Who else knows of this? If anyone hears of this, your reputation will be ruined — if it's not ruined already."

"But, Father, we didn't do anything wrong," she said, her voice quivering.

"Going out in the middle of the night with a sailor is enough!" He pointed to the window. "Get in, I say!"

From that moment on, life had been unbearable. Thanks to her father's shooting and shouting, gossip swirled around the family. Speculation ran rampant. Someone had seen Brian running from the house.

Elizabeth May's mother had simply averted her eyes in embarrassed disappointment whenever her daughter came into the room. Her father would not speak to her either; naturally, he would no longer take her to the port with him. There was no way for her to contact Brian, even though she thought of him constantly.

She felt as though she might die if she could never see him again.

It was shortly thereafter that Charles Wheldon had visited with his father, an importer of goods from the colonies to London. He was in town to arrange for a shipment of tobacco and to be introduced by his father to London Society.

Mr. Harrington had moved quickly to foster the match, inviting Charles and his father over frequently and ordering Elizabeth May to present herself in a favorable light. When Charles had finally proposed, Elizabeth May had accepted as a way to get as far away as possible from her tattered reputation, her disapproving parents, and all memory of Brian.

Now she looked up at Charles, almost having forgotten that he was there glowering at her, arms folded, waiting for her explanation. "Someone gave them to me long ago and I treat them as a keepsake. He is long gone, never to return."

They heard someone open the front door. Charles's eyes darted toward the sound, but he didn't move.

"If he is gone, then this token of his love should be gone as well." He put the earrings in his inside jacket pocket. "I will go out tonight and dispose of them for you."

"No. You cannot. They are mine!" Elizabeth May protested. As she spoke the words, they had an echo in her head. She heard herself shrieking: *Mine! Mine!*

She did not know where this other voice came from but she knew it was now her own.

The room swirled around her.

"Mine!" she screamed. It arose from somewhere so deep within. All reason and restraint left her.

She sprang from her chair. Miss Pritchard's books clattered to the floor from under her cloak.

Lunging at him, she raked his face with her nails. "Give them to me. They're mine!"

Stunned, he staggered backward.

The earrings dropped from his hands and she fell upon them, scooping them into the neckline of her dress.

Abby raced into the kitchen, pointing to Elizabeth May. Two men were right behind her. "See her! She's a witch! This proves it! Look what she's done to him!"

Elizabeth May sat crouched there, her hair loosened, blood dripping from her fingers.

The men grabbed her at each arm, dragging her to her feet.

"She . . . she attacked me," Charles stammered.

Abby crossed to the books, opening one of them to the first page. Miss Pritchard's name was written there on a book plate. "As if any further proof were needed, here it is," she announced to the men, presenting the open book triumphantly. "She's apprenticed herself to the old witch and her servant, the ones you just arrested. It's fortunate that I was there to alert you to the third member of their wicked party."

"Is this true, sir?" one of the men asked. "Do you believe your wife to be a witch?"

Charles touched his face and then gazed at the blood that smeared his hand. His eyes cut to Abby holding the books.

Elizabeth May saw what was about to happen. In a flash of understanding, she realized the maid's part in it all. "I am no witch!" she protested. "This woman wants me out of the way so she can marry my husband."

The men looked to Abby. "That's a lie," she said. "A lie told by a witch."

"Who is lying, sir?" the man asked.

Elizabeth May's black cat jumped onto the kitchen table. With one leap, it sprang into her arms, stretching up to lick her cheek.

Abby sat on the stairs, listening to the ticking grandfather clock. She wore her best dress. Her hair was neatly curled and pinned back.

Helen approached, her face swollen from crying. "I can't believe they will really burn that poor girl. They've never burned anyone for being a witch before."

"She brought it on herself," Abby said dully.

"But to be burned alive!"

Abby sniffed. "She's not the first. She won't be the last."

"How could Mr. Wheldon be there to watch?"

"He set his heart against her because she was an unfaithful witch."

"She was not!"

"Who am I to say she was not when Mr. Wheldon, a

lawyer, says otherwise? That is what he told the judge at her trial, and so it must be," Abby replied. "She fell under the sway of that Miss Pritchard and her witch slave who will burned alongside her. That's why witches must be gotten rid of, they harm and corrupt the innocent. You should have seen her that night in the kitchen. She was wild with the witchery in her."

"I can't picture it," Helen insisted.

"I saw it myself."

The door opened and Charles entered, appearing ashen and exhausted. Abby sprang to her feet as Helen retreated to the kitchen. "Let me take your coat, sir," Abby said, sliding it from his back. "Shall I bring you tea in your study?"

"Yes, please."

She made the tea, serving it to him on a silver tray. "How did it go, sir?" she asked.

His head dropped into his hands and he began to sob. "There, there," Abby soothed, putting her hands on his shoulders.

"I am so filled with guilt," he sobbed.

"You did the right thing."

"Did I?" he asked, suddenly lifting his head to her. "Or did I simply want to be rid of her?"

"No. You're an honorable man," Abby insisted. "Was it very horrible?"

He nodded. "I almost couldn't bear it. Just before they were to light the fire, I nearly came forward and said I was mistaken, that I was wrong about everything."

"What stopped you?" Abby asked.

"I realized that she was wearing those earrings. It was remarkable how they gleamed in the firelight."

Then

Before they lit the fire, as I stood at the stake beside
Miss Pritchard and Lily, I believed Brian would come
for me. He would spring from the crowd, untie my bonds,
and off we would go on a white horse. Miss Pritchard's
card reading had foretold that I would see him again.
I wore the earrings to show him that my love was still
alive, so he would know.

He did not appear.

When they lit the fire, something snapped in my
mind, cracked.

It remains broken.

My death. I do not want to talk about it.

I am smoke now, perpetually escaping from the
flame.

(On the Wheel of Rebirth)

Salem, Massachusetts, 1750:

Here lies Abigail Wheldon
1670–1750
Died of smallpox in the 80th year of her life
"As I am now, so shall ye be."
Widow of Charles Wheldon of Salem, Massachusetts
Mrs. Wheldon was the proprietor of the
Wheldon tobacco plantation. Though she comes
home to Salem for her final rest, she is no
doubt mourned by her many slaves back in Virginia.

Dublin, Ireland, 1695:

from the diary of Mrs. Brian Kelly

The baby was born while my husband was away on yet another
long sea voyage. She had her father's hazel green eyes. I named
her Maureen. All seemed fine with her until I lit a peat fire to
keep her warm. The poor babe began to scream hysterically. I
nursed her and rocked her and did all in my power to soothe

the pathetic wailing creature but she would have none of it. I was so distracted that I forgot to attend the fire and let it die down. Only then did little Maureen stop crying.

After that she slept a great deal and was a good baby, except when I lit the fire. Each time she would fall into a fit of pitiful crying. I could not keep the fire unlit as it is the dead of winter and we would freeze without it, though now I wish I had done without and taken my chances under woolen blankets. One night it was so cold everywhere in our thatched cottage that I sat beside the fire, rocking the wee babe in my arms, enduring her nerve-racking screams.

I fell asleep and when I awoke, the baby was dead in my arms. The doctor says she most likely died of smoke fumes. I believe she died of fear and I blame myself for leaving her near the flame for so long. For the life of me, I can't imagine why a child should be born with a wild terror of flames such as that, but that she had it, I am certain.

My heart is broken. Her father, Brian, comes home from sea today. I don't know how I will tell him his baby girl is gone.

Rosetta, Egypt, July 1799:

To My Rosalie,
As you know, since we first set sail on 19 April 1798 under the command of the great Napoleon Bonaparte so much has happened. The city of Alexandria, which we successfully

conquered in the name of France during the Battle of the Pyramids last July, has seen great improvements under French rule. Streetlights have been installed, hospitals have been established, and the lawless citizens have been disarmed, among many other improvements.

These things, however, are not what I want to tell you. In other letters I have imparted the sensations that have come over me since arriving in this exotic country. Things that should be wholly unfamiliar are strangely known to me. When we fought against the troops of the Egyptian governor last year, I could hardly fire my gun, so overcome was I with the feeling that I had been there before. At first, the old headaches returned, so frightening and unexplainable were these sensations.

And now, just yesterday, the most bizarre of all occurrences happened. In a city known to us as Rosetta, though the natives call it Rashid, on the west bank of the formidable Nile River, my company was working under the direction of Captain Pierre Francois Xavier Bouchard, an able leader. We were engaged in the task of knocking down an old wall to extend Fort Julien, our base of operation. I was about to demolish a wall with a sledgehammer when I noticed that there was writing inscribed on the wall. It was a text etched in three different languages. You know I speak and write only one language, French, but this is the curious part: I could read most of this ancient inscription.

It was written in Greek, and in Egyptian hieroglyphics, and

I could read them both. The third script, below the other two, I could not read, although it appeared to be Egyptian of some kind. The hieroglyphics and the Greek said the same thing. They were thanking one of the ptolemies, who I am told were Greek pharaohs of Egypt, for something.

I called over Captain Bouchard to tell him what I had discovered. "That is impossible," he said. "No one can understand the meaning behind this ancient picture language of the Egyptians. How do you know this?"

I confessed that I was as bewildered by it as he; nonetheless, I was certain my reading was accurate. Still skeptical, the captain preserved the piece of writing and had it presented to the scholars who have accompanied Napoleon here to Egypt. They are studying it now.

After this, my dreams have been filled with strange imagery. I see myself shooting arrows and a pulsing green eye hovers in a black, star-flecked sky. Last night I dreamed I rowed up the Nile in an ancient boat with many other men. Whips snapped over our heads.

I suppose these fevered dreams are to be expected here in this foreign land. Though I long to see you again, part of me will always belong to Egypt.

Sincerely,
Jacques

Bedlam Hospital, London,
September 1810: Case 781

By order of the asylum administrator, Mr. Phineas Smith, the unfortunate Marianna Clark will heretofore be bound by hand and foot and strapped to a chair during the waking hours. This has been deemed necessary because Miss Clark remains under a delusion that has been with her since birth: She believes that she is on fire.

Until last week, this condition would arise only under stressful situation calling for short-term confinement. The condition appeared to be worsening with the result that Miss Clark believed she was ablaze at almost every waking hour.

Under these dire conditions I recommended that Miss Clark be administered the potent opium derivative known as laudanum in order to calm her. However, in this sedated state, Miss Clark claims with utmost certainty to be someone called the Mother Abbess Maria Regina, continually insisting, "This is my abbey. I know this building but someone has moved my room! Where is my room?" This claim would simply seem to be the further ravings of an unfortunate lunatic but it has an uncanny dimension to it. This very hospital building where the miserable Miss Clark is now incarcerated had its beginnings in the Middle Ages as a priory for the Catholic brothers and sisters of the Order of the Star of Bethlehem. In all likelihood, Miss Clark read this information during more lucid moments between her stays here and recalls it now in her delirium.

It is my considered opinion that it is in everyone's best interest for Miss Clark, in addition to being bound hand and foot, to be given daily a greatly increased dosage of laudanum. This will calm her and reduce her shrieking and the demented claims, which greatly unnerve the staff.

New York City, 1863

Dear George,

How are you? I hope things have been calm down there in Gettysburg. Guess what? A man offered me three hundred dollars to take his place in the army and I took it. Now you won't be the only soldier!

Jane yelled for an hour when I came home and told her. She was glad for the three hundred dollars, and simmered down when I showed it to her.

When I came out of the foundling home at sixteen, she was the only one I knew, since we grew up in the home together. She was like a sister to me and I always liked her beautiful red curls. Marrying her seemed like the sensible thing to do. She told me it was, though now I deeply regret it.

So that was part of the reason I needed to get away. She was driving me crazy. I hear Mr. Lincoln also has a tiresome, crazy wife, so I guess it's not just the poor who are afflicted with such.

The other reason I needed to get out was that these tenements are near to driving me insane. Every other day there's a fire in one of them. These old wooden buildings go up in a second. They're so overcrowded that someone is always accidentally knocking over a lamp or leaving a stove flame on, not to mention the drunkards who pass out with lit cigarettes still burning.

As if all this isn't bad enough, it's part of my duties to fire up that new kiln in Pfeiffer's Pottery Shop where I work. I was happy enough to get the job for, as you well know, I love making the pots like they taught us at the orphanage. The kiln shoots jets of fire just outside the building. I can see the flames through the window. Each time I see the flame jumping up, I nearly faint from terror. Jane says that I'm like a crazy person about fire but I can't help it.

That's probably why I started taking the laudanum, my nerves being shot from my fear of fire. I got a doctor to get it for me to treat my bad ankle, which still gives out on me at the worst times. I hope it doesn't give me a problem during the fighting — my ankle I mean, not the laudanum. To be totally honest, I look forward to taking the laudanum as it more or less puts me in another world.

Well, maybe I'll run into you. I hope so. The only thing I'll miss from my present life is my cat, who I call Baby. He's the pottery shop's cat, really, but I've made him my pet. I don't suppose pets are allowed in the army. I can tell you that I'm exceedingly happy to be getting out of here.

Your brother,
John

The Battle of Honey Springs, Indian Territory, July 17, 1863

John Mays looked across the field from which he'd just come. The Confederate soldiers were still in their line, muskets at the ready, but they'd sat down to rest.

Looking around, he gazed over miles of rolling hills dotted with stands of trees and a river. He'd seen more countryside in the last six months than in his entire life spent in the city, but he had never expected that the fighting would take him this far away. Honey Springs wasn't even in a state. It was Indian Territory.

This battle had been going on for over an hour and the Confederate infantry forces under General Douglas Cooper were tough. And they weren't only the regular rebel troops, either; they had independent Texas regiments and the Indians fighting with them. Some Cherokee were fighting with the north; Choctaw, Creek, Chickasaw, and Seminole were all fighting with the South. The Indians called this area Elk Creek.

He was already exhausted. They'd marched all night through the rain to get to the fort. Plus, he was out of laudanum, which was bad. He hadn't realized how much he'd come to depend on it. Without the stuff, he really felt like death.

The Union cavalry soldiers on horseback milled together not far away. Like the foot soldiers, they were temporarily resting themselves and their horses, readying to return to battle.

John didn't know if he could go back into battle again. His ankle, which had always been weak, now throbbed. Yanking up his pant leg, he saw that it had swollen to more than twice its usual size. It had started to hurt during the long walk last night and he'd turned it during the first advance, but still he'd pushed himself to keep going. Now he stood and his ankle instantly buckled under, dropping him down onto one knee.

He was still down when he saw a line of fresh Union infantry troops march past him, advancing on the enemy. They were African soldiers! Some of them might have been freeborn, especially out here in the territories, but others of them had to be freed slaves. "Who are they?" he asked a nearby soldier.

"Kansas First Regiment," the soldier answered. His cartridge pouch was out and he was reloading his musket. "All volunteer colored infantry under James Lane."

"Can they fight?" he asked.

The soldier shrugged. "I sure hope so."

John's regiment was ordered to stand their ground as skirmishers, taking on any rebel troops that broke through the line. Meanwhile the African soldiers, with aid from the Cherokee, advanced on the enemy straight on.

The Kansas First marched to within fifty paces of the

Confederates and opened fire. They exchanged a volley of gunfire that filled the air with smoke.

Lou Jones was at the front of the Union line, her musket pointed forward, ready. With her black hair cut short and her slim, athletic physique, she looked like a boy, a soldier boy. In her Union gray uniform, nobody but she knew any different. The rain had begun coming down hard now. Her uniform was heavy. Even if it got soaked, it wouldn't cling and give her away. But she would have to reload soon and she was concerned about her gunpowder getting wet.

Between the driving rain and the gray, gunpowder-thick air, she couldn't see much. She shot straight ahead, into the enemy line, letting her ears guide her.

Crouching there on the field, she drew a cartridge from the supply case slung over her shoulder. As she'd been trained to do, she bit off the part of the paper cartridge that held the bullet. Clasping the bullet between her teeth, she cocked the gun and poured some of the powder from the cartridge into the priming pan.

She was about to spit the bullet into the gun barrel and ram it down with the ramrod attached to the musket when a Cherokee warrior came flying off his horse, hurtling through the air. Before she could dodge, he crashed on top of her as his horse ran off wildly into the field.

Rolling out from under the dead man, she scrambled for her gun, which lay cocked, several feet away.

A rebel soldier stepped in front of her, blocking the path to the gun. Looking up, his hate-filled eyes blazed down at her as he lifted his gun to fire.

She knew that face.

A flush of humiliation and rage overcame her. One of her terrible headaches was threatening, beginning to throb in the right-hand corner of her temple.

No! she commanded it. She could not be disabled by a headache at this moment.

This man before her would not win. "Not this time!" she shouted at him as she scooped up the bow and quiver of arrows that the fallen Cherokee had flung to the ground. With a knowledge seemingly born in her body, she deftly, fluidly loaded the bow and shot the arrow at the rebel soldier.

His gun went off, ripping the skin from her forehead as he staggered backward.

Blood pouring down her face, Lou grabbed for her gun and stood. The soldier lay in the field on his stomach.

And then he moaned, not dead!

Her gun was not yet reloaded so she grabbed another arrow, positioned it, and drew the bow, aiming down at him.

It was her moment to finish him.

But, strangely, she felt no desire to do it.

Coming to consciousness, he rolled around. His eyes widened as he looked up and saw her there. It was at that moment she realized the Confederate infantry, the Texas regiment, and the Indian troops were retreating, fleeing the field.

The rebel she had cornered raced away, clutching his shoulder with the arrow still jutting from it.

She could have easily hit him again, but she lowered her bow. Watching them run from the field, she felt fully satisfied.

The field doctor had sent John down to the river to soak his ankle in the icy running water. He put his hand on his musket, sensing someone's approach, but relaxed when he saw it was only a soldier from the Kansas First Regiment. He was a young soldier, thin with not yet even the trace of a beard. John guessed he had lied about his age in order to join his regiment.

"Your men fought well out there today," he complimented the soldier. "After this battle, there can be no doubt that you men are fine soldiers. I heard General Blunt say so himself. I think he's going to write as much in his report, too."

The young soldier nodded. John could see that his face was covered in dried blood. A horrific purple gash crossed his forehead. Whatever he'd been through, he was no doubt lucky to be alive. The soldier crouched by the stream a few yards away and began to splash his face with water, washing the caked blood from his face.

John pushed himself up and hobbled to the boy. "That's a nasty-looking gash on your forehead," he commented. He pulled a clean handkerchief from his inside pocket. "Here, take this. It will make the job easier."

"Thanks," the young soldier mumbled, soaking the handkerchief in the river.

John sat beside him, feeling oddly comfortable, perhaps because they had just come through such an ordeal together. He was surprised at his level of ease. He had never met a colored person before, though he'd seen some slaves and freeborn artisans in the city. He'd never actually spoken to someone from another race other than his own.

"How'd you come to join your regiment?" John asked, picking up a lump of mud from the riverbank and squeezing it absently. Its cold wetness was soothing in his rough hand, like the wet clay in Pfeiffer's Pottery Shop.

"Just volunteered," the young soldier answered, looking away. "Seemed like the right thing to do."

"You freeborn or slave-born?" John asked.

The boy's eyes narrowed suspiciously. "Freeborn," he answered, standing. "Mind if I keep the handkerchief for a while?" He pressed it to his wound.

"Sure. Keep it," John answered.

"Thanks." The young soldier hurried off and John had the feeling he couldn't get away fast enough.

In her small tent within the fort courtyard, Lou listened to the silence in her head. Despite the ache in her bloodied forehead, the high whine of headache pain she'd grown accustomed to was not present.

She dared not even breathe or move, fearing that the slightest change in her position would bring the headaches scorching back.

Steeling her nerves, she turned her head, first to the right, then to the left.

No pain.

Since birth she'd suffered the worst headaches — blinding pain that nauseated her, made light itself splinter into shards. Any kind of hardship or upset would bring it on.

But now she had no pain — at least not in her head.

Her side was hot, though, right at her lower abdomen. It wasn't her time of month; that had passed. It was something else and it wasn't right. Unbuckling her pants, she pushed them down, revealing the blue-black birthmark at her side, the one that her mama said looked like a stab wound. She poked her side tenderly. Ow!

After a moment of lying there, breathing deeply, the pain subsided enough that she felt able to go out to get food.

Outside in the courtyard, the men were up and about, eating the chipped beef being served by the regimental cooks at a long, rough-hewn table. A bonfire roared at the center of the courtyard, turning the men into dark silhouettes with the occasional vivid face jumping into clarity as a soldier was illuminated by the flame.

There was boisterous singing of off-color ditties. Uproarious laughter exploded into the night. High spirits over the day's victory overpowered any fatigue.

Lou smiled and nodded at the others in her regiment as she loaded her plate. Usually, the Kansas First Regiment ate a bit away from the others, never knowing what kind of reception they'd receive from the white soldiers, and preferring the ease they experienced only among one another.

It was different for Lou, though. She remained aloof even among her own regiment. None of these men suspected that she was female, and that was how it had to stay.

Tonight the Kansas First seemed to have dropped much of their wary guard. Earlier, General Blunt had praised their courage and military skill in front of all the regiments. Now they laughed and joked with the white soldiers, who in turn praised them with high spirits.

They were drinking beer, and soon General Blunt's assistant appeared with an oak barrel of whiskey. This was met with an uproar of cheering.

Lou accepted the whiskey that was poured into her tin mess cup, but discreetly poured it into the dirt at her feet. Letting the whiskey ease her into an unguarded moment could have disastrous consequences.

After a few rowdy songs by members of the cavalry, the Kansas First soldiers were called upon to sing. They began a spiritual called "Swing Lo, Sweet Chariot." A lot of the other soldiers knew it and sang along.

While they were singing, Lou felt thirsty and searched for something nonalcoholic to drink. Remembering a pump she'd seen back by the fort's outer wall, she left the warmth of the bonfire to pick her way through the shadows to get some water.

In the darkness by the pump she was quickly aware of an even darker form a few feet away. He was vomiting violently onto the ground.

She quickly pumped some water into her tin cup and brought it to him. "Hey, have this," she offered.

The sick man was the same soldier she'd met down by the river. Wiping his mouth with his sleeve, he gulped from the cup and spit into the dirt. "Thanks."

"Hope it wasn't that chipped beef," she said with a hearty laugh. "I just finished a plate of it."

He shook his head. "No. It's the fire. It's part of the problem, anyway."

"The fire?"

He sat down heavily on a rough-hewn bench close by. "I'm scared to death of it, always have been. I'm also out of the stuff I take for the pain in my ankle. Laudanum."

"What happened to the ankle?"

"Nothing. It's always been a bum ankle. The laudanum is supposed to help the pain. I've been on the stuff so long that being without it is making me real sick."

"Ask the doctor for some," she suggested.

"I did. He said he wished he had some. He's amputating

legs with only whiskey to give guys for the pain. When he hears Blunt gave some of the whiskey out tonight, he's gonna have a fit."

She nodded somberly, having witnessed field hospital conditions and knowing the atrocities.

"You're a runaway slave, aren't you?" John said.

"Yeah, I ran away," she heard herself say, as though the words were coming from someone else's mouth. The Fugitive Slave Act had been repealed last year and slaves no longer had to be returned to their owners, but admitting to being a runaway still made her nervous.

"I had a feeling," he replied. "You didn't seem too at ease talking to me back there by the river. How'd you do it?"

She chuckled bitterly. "You're going to hate this. I was working in the house and I set the drapes on fire. While everyone was busy stomping on the fire, I slipped out the back door. It was so simple, I could hardly believe it."

"You were lucky," he commented.

"Lucky, and I had help. I made it to the Ohio River by night. A former slave now living free in Ohio rowed out and brought me over."

"Have you seen a lot of fighting?" the man asked.

She shook her head. "Up to now, we've been used as escort troops, mostly. We were attacked by Texas troops with some Seminole while escorting a supply train here to the fort. We sent them running, so I guess the general felt okay about calling us in today. This was our first real official fight."

Although the night was cool, the other soldier was sweating profusely. "How did it feel out there today?" he asked, wiping his brow with his sleeve.

She reflected on this a moment before answering. To fight full out — what a release! To no longer bite down on murderous rage as she'd done in her role as slave. She'd felt wildly free during the fight at the train and again today. And yet, as she'd watched the other side retreat off the battlefield, something in her had shifted. She was aware of it though she couldn't quite name the feeling. "I felt sorry for them," she said at last.

The soldier let out a harsh laugh. "Don't. It will cripple you. You'll be no good to anybody. I used to be full of empathy but this war has knocked it out of me. And you know what? It feels good not to care."

"You don't care for anyone?" she questioned.

It was his turn to reflect. "No. I don't think so ... my brother, maybe, but who knows where he is right now. How about you?"

"My mother was sold downriver before I made a run for it. If we win this war, or even if we don't, I'm going to try to find her. Other than her, I have no one."

"I have a wife, but to tell the truth, I don't miss her. In fact, it's been a relief to be without her these days. If there's one good thing that's come to me from this war, that's it."

Since she'd taken on this male disguise, it had been interesting to talk to men without the barrier between men and women standing in the way — the polite or not so polite flirtation, the unspoken implication that there was so much out there in the world that was beyond her understanding. All that was swept aside when she began dressing as a man.

It astounded her how easily she took to life as a man; she felt entirely comfortable in the male role at most times. Although her former slave life had been harsh, as a house slave she'd been spared the rigors of the fields and cast into the feminine role of cook's helper. It had been hard work but she accomplished it all within the guidelines of polite female comportment. She would have thought these things were ingrained in her, yet she had thrown them all off with ease. She'd even learned to spit freely without feeling self-conscious, even discovering that she was quite good at it.

This ability to assume a male role was, in a way, akin to her mysterious skill with a bow and arrow.

Where had that come from?

Of course, she had watched the Cherokee warriors closely, fascinated by their prowess with the bow. It was strange that the ability had found its way into her body, for that was how it had felt, like a skill that bypassed her brain and came straight from her spine, arms, and hands. It had saved her life out there on the field.

The sound of the singing Kansas First drifted on the air. Their song was now "Amazing Grace."

"I love this song," Lou said.

"I do, too. It was written by a former British slaver who gave up slaving after a near shipwreck. I learned it in the orphanage." He lifted his sweat-moist face as a faraway look filled his eyes. He sang along with the distant voices of the Kansas First.

His voice was full, rich, and deep. While he sang, his sweating cleared, his hands stopped trembling. An other-worldly light radiated from his face. Lou sat, transfixed, gooseflesh rising on her arms at the sound of his singing. He seemed transported, as was she, into some other realm.

When the song ended, he smiled fleetingly, a little embarrassed at having given himself over to the rapture of the music. "It's a good song," he muttered.

"It is," she agreed. "You sing it well."

With a quick nod, he brushed off the compliment. "What will you do after the war?" John asked.

"After I find my mother and get her to safety, I'd like to write a book, tell a story about everything I've seen," she admitted, then laughed at her own lofty aspiration. "First thing I'll have to do is learn to write, of course. What are your intentions? You should sing on the stage."

"In the city, I sneaked into the opera once and watched from the sides. I liked it but it's not for a poor man like me. I was thinking of starting my own pottery shop, like the one I used to work for in New York City. People are always going to need cups, bowls, and plates, and I love to work the pottery wheel."

"Don't you need to put fire on it?" Lou asked.

"Yep. But I'm determined to get over this fear of fire. I feel it is the one thing I must do before I die. And I probably should try to kick this addiction to the laudanum."

"Addiction?" Lou asked. She didn't know the word.

"I'm so dependent on the stuff. I can't live without it." He had begun sweating again. He nodded toward his badly quivering hands. "How can I fire my musket when I'm like this?"

Lou nodded. "We have to get you some of that laudanum. I think that there was some on the supply train we escorted in." She nodded for him to follow her. She knew exactly where the crates had been stacked.

Alone in his tent, John snapped open one of the glass phials of laudanum Lou had found for him. What an odd guy Lou was, so delicate and yet so gutsy. Together, under the cover of darkness, they'd cracked open a crate of the drug and loaded themselves with as many glass phials as they could carry.

As they were getting away, Lou had buckled over and clutched his side. When John asked what was wrong, he'd insisted it was nothing. He hoped the kid was all right. It was strange how he felt so at ease with him, so comfortable, especially considering how different they were. It was as though Lou was some long-lost brother John had been reunited with, instead of a stranger whose former life he couldn't even begin to imagine.

He sure owed Lou a lot for finding this laudanum.

With badly shaking hands, John brought the greenish brown liquid to his lips. The bitter taste suffused him with warm relief. Lying flat on his bedroll, he waited for the familiar relaxing sensation to wash over him. This phial held more than he usually took, but he'd been so long without it that he didn't care and finished the entire thing.

He had never before taken so much that it brought on hallucinations, and so he was unprepared for what happened next.

His body lifted out of his tent, serenely happy to be floating above the earth in the night sky. One star was brighter than the others and kept growing increasingly brighter. As it came closer, a giant bird flew out of the brightness. It held Lou in its talons, his legs dangling, and his face joyful.

An explosion of yellow light obliterated everything and suddenly he was traveling at full speed through desert sands. He was singing "Amazing Grace" beside a crystal blue pool abundant with floating lotus flowers. Lou walked next to the pool wearing his Union uniform. He was captive of a Confederate soldier. John's wife Jane was there, pouring beer from a jug for members of the audience.

His eyes fixed on Lou. He waited for Lou to tell him

something but Lou didn't seem able to talk. John continued to sing and his voice became much higher than he recognized.

He saw himself in the pool's reflection. He had become a woman with thick black hair.

How had he disappeared like this?

He found himself again, sitting on a small boat in a murky river surrounded with fog. An old man stood at the bow. Looking over the side of the boat, he saw a pair of green gemstone earrings, hooked one to the other. Without stopping to think, he went over the side to get them.

In the water, his long, tangled hair floated out around him. Lou was swimming toward him. He was in his uniform but his jaw jutted forward, his brow sloped. He was Lou but different.

They were both swimming toward the green earrings.

The earrings swirled.

A turquoise Eye of Horus formed around the green gems.

The Eye of Horus spun so fast it became a glistening green orb.

Lou wrapped his hand around it. John grasped just as tight. Both clutching the stone, struggling for it, they shot out of the water straight up into the starry night. . . .

John's eyes snapped open and he shook, his teeth chattering. Someone had hurled a bucket of ice water at him. He lay on a cot in a tent with the sides tied up. He was strapped to the cot with rope.

"Wake up, soldier!" the tall, lanky field doctor barked, untying the rope. He was the same doctor John had asked for laudanum days earlier, the one with the eye patch over one eye. "I don't know where you got all that laudanum but we need this cot for soldiers with real injuries."

John's mouth was like a wool blanket. All his muscles ached.

"You raved for a full day before we could get hold of you," the doctor reported. "You've been here for two more. That's as much as we can spare for a drug addict. By the way, don't go looking for that laudanum. You're on your way to being free of it now; you don't want to go back. Besides, we confiscated what we found in your tent."

"Water, please," John murmured.

The doctor poured some water from a pitcher into a cup and handed it to him. Anguished cries of injured soldiers could be heard from the other tents. "In fact," the doctor went on, "we couldn't give you more even if we wanted to. We've used up the small supply they sent us, just in the last three days alone."

A terrible moan came from the next tent over. "I wish I had some for that poor soul," the doctor remarked. "Ruptured appendix."

John staggered to the back of the tent and looked over. "Lou," he gasped softly.

"You know him?" the doctor asked. "Or should I say, her?"

John whirled sharply toward the doctor. *"Her?"*

The doctor nodded. "Young women disguised as soldiers: It's not the first time I've seen it in this war — young women following a sweetheart, looking for adventure, wanting to serve the cause. If you can lend her some comfort, go ahead, 'cause she's not going to make it."

"Hey," Lou said softly when he came into her tent. "You okay? You don't look so good."

"I'm all right," he replied, sitting at the side of her bed. "How do you feel?"

"Like death. The pain in my gut is awful."

He nodded. "Can I get you anything?"

"You could promise me something. It's a lot to ask but I don't have anyone else."

"What?"

"My mother's name is Eva Jones. She's in Mississippi somewhere. The North is going to win this war. Afterward, would you try to find her and see that she's all right? Help her if she needs help."

"I promise," he replied.

Pain made her press her lips together hard. "Don't have any of that laudanum, do you?"

As though suddenly remembering something, he reached into his pants pocket and pulled out a nearly empty phial. At the bottom was a tiny puddle, mere drops, of the drug.

He held it up. A crack of sunlight shafting down from

a tear in the tent roof caught the edge of the glass phial. It threw a prism of green and yellow against the tent wall.

Eyeing it hungrily for a moment, he wrapped his hand around it, killing the prism.

"That green light was pretty. Put it back," she requested.

"I'll give it to you for the pain," he offered.

"Not yet," she said. "I want to look at it while you tell me a story." She had discovered that staring at the green prism distracted her from the pain, eased her mind somehow.

"What kind of story would you like?"

"Anything at all that I can listen to while I look at this green light, just to keep my mind off the pain."

"I can't think of a story."

"Tell me a story about two friends who just met but feel like they've known each other for a long time."

"All right. I'll make it up as I go along." He held the phial up to the sunlight, and the greenish yellow prism once again appeared on the tent wall. He peered into it as if, somehow, the story lay within.

"There once was a girl who lived in ancient Greece. She hated her boring life there. She longed for adventure and freedom. One day she met a wild boy in the woods. He was hunting with a bow and arrow on her father's property. The moment she looked at him, she felt that she had known him all her life, that he was somehow a part of her and always would be."

"That's nice," she said. It was exactly how she'd felt when she spoke to him there by the pump the other night. That night seemed like a lifetime ago. It was before he'd fallen into a laudanum-induced delirium, before her appendix had erupted in agony. "Go on," she prompted in a weak voice, her eyes still fixed on the green prism.

"The girl wanted the boy to come win her hand in marriage," he continued. "She was sure he'd come because the connection between them had been so strong. She was sure he loved her as much as she loved him."

"He did," she murmured, not sure how she knew it.

"Then why didn't he come for her?"

"He was hurt. A rival for her affection had beat him up and left him for dead."

"He wanted to come then?" John asked.

"Yes," she said. It was as if she was speaking from somewhere deep and mysterious within her mind, saying things she knew were true. "And he came for her in the end, didn't he? He gave her earrings to promise his love."

"In the end," John said, "she went to him."

"She wasn't going to him. She threw the earrings he'd given her away. She didn't love him," Lou corrected him.

"The girl *did* love him," John insisted. "Someone else threw the earrings. She was trying to get them so he wouldn't misunderstand."

"But the wild boy had seen the earrings fall and he was after them, too. He wanted to insist that she take them back," Lou said. She could see it all. The glistening stone in the moonlight, like the prism on the wall — two hands reaching out for it. "Then what happened?" she asked.

"I don't know how it ends," John said.

"You must know. It's your story," Lou reminded him. "You say she didn't throw the earrings away?"

"No. Someone else did. She loved him very much," John told her. "She couldn't stand to be without him any longer."

"She *did* love him," Lou repeated, turning the sound of the words over in her mind. *She did love him.* "I never knew that," she whispered.

"Want that laudanum now?"

"No, this green light is enough." Her eyes were drifting shut but she forced them open, not wanting to take her gaze away. "She loved him, you say?"

Then

I am suddenly all better. Not only has the pain left my body but my mind is strangely glad as I step out of my lifeless shell.

I am done with this life of slavery, no longer a fugitive.

Leaving the tent, I walk around. Members of my regiment are coming to see me. They don't yet know that I was female. I hope I can stay long enough to see the looks on their faces.

They are good men. I love them as brothers. In fact, I recognize one somehow. The name Ato comes to mind. And the name Aken, too.

It is this Ato now who stands outside my tent and talks to the doctor. He looks shocked at first. I listen in as he tells the others I have died. "Lou was a brave soldier," he says to them, never revealing my secret.

The others bow their heads and murmur their agreement. Good-bye, Kansas First Regiment. I was proud to serve with you. Perhaps we will meet again.

I return to John sitting beside my cot, weeping. We have shared a strong bond, too soon broken. The story he has just told me is important. It has a meaning to me that I do not understand, but it has left me with great peace of mind.

I think it has to do with something I have forgotten. My mind struggles to remember what it could be.

I can't remember. I wish he would tell the story again. I feel I could listen to it a hundred times.

But he is fading away. In a moment's time everything has become blurred.

My regiment begins to softly sing "Swing Lo, Sweet Chariot" by my body.

Oh, I don't want to go.

I'm afraid to forget all I have just come to know.

I was taught to fear God and to want heaven. I can't want it now, I'm not ready. Too much of me longs for this green, green earth; all the beauty, even the sadness and heartbreak.

The tents of the field hospital are now faded, like a sun-bleached design on old drapery. I raise my arms. "I don't want to go!" I wail, though no sound comes from my mouth. "Let me stay!"

The scene transforms and I am on a cloud. I am standing in front of a tall, white, gleaming gate. I knock but no one answers. I wait so long that I become tired and sit down in front of the gate, resting my back against it.

I sleep and crash through many dreams. Images flash

in front of me: pyramids, statues, sailing ships, men in chains, people I have loved, those I have wronged, things I have won, things I have lost.

I answer questions.

Was this good? Yes.

Would you change that? No.

What did you need then?

Did you get it?

What do you need now?

What must you learn?

How can you get it?

Choose.

Choose.

Choose.

I awaken, still in front of the gate. I cannot remember my name or where I have come from or anything that has ever happened to me.

"When will I see the face of God?" I ask out loud.

I hear the answer almost as if a voice speaks in my head.

Not yet.

A column of white light appears before me. It soars upward and is accompanied by a deep, vibrating hum.

I have seen this before but cannot recall where or when I encountered it. I am familiar with this shining illumination, just the same.

The low throb of its hum suffuses me until I also reverberate with an answering vibration that emanates from my core.

"You are an angel," I say, looking up into its translucent face, seeing its enormous feathered wings, and somehow knowing this is true. "What is your name?"

"I am the archangel Michael," it replies in a voice so resounding I must cover my ears. "I am The Hinge of the Universe."

It spreads its blinding white wings. I heed this invitation and walk into its light.

(On the Wheel of Rebirth)

Boston, Massachusetts, 1915:

Mr. and Mrs. Robert Brody announced the arrival of their new bundle of joy, an eight-pound, bouncing baby boy, born yesterday. Baby and mother are doing just fine. The proud papa told us: "He'll be Robert Brody the Fourth, but we intend to call him Bert."

Paris, 1937

Delilah Jones stroked the panther's sleek black coat. "You're on in ten, Miss Jones," the stage manager called to the Panther Club's headliner.

"Thanks," she replied, rising from her dressing room chair. She adjusted the straps of her tight red satin halter-dress so it would reveal more of her cocoa-colored skin. As she threw on her white, pleated cape, tying it at the neck, she set her golden cobra headdress carefully atop her black curls. She hooked a leash onto her pet panther's emerald-studded collar. "Come on, Baby," she said to it. "Let's you and me strut our stuff."

The panther strained at the leash as she walked through the narrow backstage hallways. Together, they waited in the wings. From the brightly lit stage, the club's owner, a man with movie-star polish in a well-tailored tux, announced her: "All the way from the jazz clubs of New Orleans, here now with us in Paris — The Panther Club's very own Miss Delilah Jones!"

The lights went out while Del silently walked Baby to center stage. Then the spotlight hit her face dramatically.

Del began her act with a high, sultry jazz whine as the light expanded to reveal her, along with Baby at her side.

The audience gasped slightly when Baby stretched her jaw, soundlessly showing off her sharp teeth as Del had taught her. Four years ago, when she was thirteen, Del had worked as an assistant in a big cat act in the circus. Baby had been the runt of the panther litter and would have been put to sleep if Del hadn't claimed her as her own. Now she was as docile as a kitten, but the audience didn't know that.

Once the audience had recovered from the sight of Baby, Del spread her arms, fanning her cape so that it revealed how shapely and stunning she looked in her dress. Her song began with a sultry glide across the stage. "If you find your-self on the River Nile and you're sorely in need of a reason to smile . . . ," she crooned as she dropped the cape to the ground. The headpiece came off next while the band kicked into high gear. "Just call me Isis, I'm the nicest on the Nile," Del belted out, arms wide. "I'm a goddess with a great sense of style. We'll find a little room in a great big mummy tomb. Desert sands may blow our way but entombed you'll want to stay . . . with Isis, the nicest on the Ni-i-i-le."

The song continued full of puns and racy jokes all centered on a comic version of ancient Egyptian life. The audience laughed at all the right places, and as she became increasingly assured that she had them, Del's voice soared as never before, growling down low in some parts and ris-ing to a hornlike peel in others. She sang the next verses in French, which guaranteed that everyone in the audience would get the jokes.

When the song was done, the audience pounded the tables, clapping, whistling, and shouting her name. While she bowed and waved to them, she made sure to stroke Baby to keep her calm.

Delilah Jones has arrived! she thought, flashing the audience a brilliant smile.

Bert Brody rapped on the dressing room door. The name Delilah Jones was scrawled across it in black marker. He needed some background and perhaps quotes for the review he was writing for *Traveling Abroad* magazine.

"Come in," a rich, alto-pitched voice responded.

Bert opened the door to find Delilah Jones wrapped in an emerald green satin kimono. By her side was the man with the great tux. Bert knew he was the club's owner, Leonard Raymond. "Tell her she was sensational," Raymond said.

"You were sensational," Bert obeyed dryly.

"Don't pass out from enthusiasm," she replied.

He laughed. "No, sorry. I mean it. You were great. Honestly. With the right songs, you could really be a star."

"What do you mean 'with the right songs'?" she shot back, her pencil-thin eyebrow arched. "And I *am* a star! I love that song. The woman who used to sing it when I traveled with vaudeville was three times my size and she had an alligator on a leash. It's even better the way I do it and with a panther. A panther is better than an alligator, don't you think? They loved it tonight, didn't they, Lenny?"

"You wowed 'em, Del," he assured her.

"See? What do you know about songs, anyway?" she challenged Bert.

"Well," he began hesitantly. "I write them and —"

"Oh, I can just imagine the kinds of songs you write! What are their titles, 'All Hail Harvard' or 'Yippee for Yale'?"

"Actually, I just graduated from Princeton."

She laughed in a way that made him glance at the bottle of champagne on her dressing room table. It was half empty and he saw that two glasses had been drained. "So I guess your song is 'Pip, Pip for Princeton!'" she said.

"Maybe this isn't a good time. I'd like to interview you, though. I'm a writer for *Traveling Abroad* magazine."

"Are you calling me a broad?" she cried. He wasn't sure if she was really offended or joking.

"No, I would never —"

"You're certainly not traveling anywhere with me, broad or not, get that idea out of your head," she went on, teasing.

"You've got it all wrong, I —"

"You're blushing!" she cackled, pointing at his face, and then screamed with laughter, rocking back on her chair.

The heat at Bert's cheeks told him she was right, and knowing it made him grow even redder. This was a disaster.

"Some other time," he mumbled, backing out of the dressing room. He heard them guffawing from behind the door as he retreated down the hall.

Utterly mortified, head down, he hurried through the cramped backstage area. He was nearly out the door when he heard light, running footsteps.

"Wait!" Turning, he saw Delilah Jones, barefoot and still in her kimono, running to him.

"I'm sorry." Breathless, she laid her hand on his arm.

He pushed the door open. "It's okay. Forget it."

"It's the champagne. It makes me think I'm a lot funnier than I really am. Meet me at the Parthenon on the Left Bank tomorrow at noon. I'll buy you a croissant and a café au lait to make it up to you. We'll do the interview then. Okay?"

He was tempted to say no; she had made a fool of him, and he didn't like it. But he wanted this story to be good. If it was, they'd throw more assignments his way. If he got regular magazine writing jobs, he could stay in Paris and try to write more songs — maybe get them put into a musical revue like the one he'd just seen. He'd show his father that he wasn't dependent on the family for money. He could make his own way.

"Please. I could use the publicity," she coaxed.

"Well, I do think you could be great with better songs," he said. "Did that woman really have an alligator?"

Delilah chuckled and looked away for a second and then up at him. "I made her up. I wrote that song."

"You did?" He could feel himself reddening again. He would have been more tactful if he'd realized the song was her own creation. "How did you ever come up with it?"

She shrugged. "The song just came to me. So did the story about the fat lady and the alligator. Things just pop into my head. I really did sing in vaudeville, though, after the circus."

"I can tell that you're an experienced performer," he conceded.

"You bet I am! And don't tell me the audience didn't love the song — because they did," she insisted.

"Yes, they did," he admitted. "The song is funny and you have a spectacular voice. You wowed 'em, as Lenny there said."

"Oh, yeah, Lenny — don't remind me," she said dismissively. "He hired me to be the next toast of Paris, the next Josephine Baker. He was just opening the club and he needed somebody fast. I talked my way into the job because I swore to him I could do it, but between us, I'm not so sure."

"You can do it," Bert said, suddenly certain this was true. "If you sing *my* songs, it will definitely happen. If you keep on with only the comic material, you'll always be a novelty act."

He braced himself for another eruption of derisive laughter. But this time she only looked up at him thoughtfully, so he dared to continue. "I've written some love songs, real sophisticated stuff. It would give you some class."

"Hey, I already have class! What makes you think you know so much, College Boy?" she asked defensively.

"I've been to Broadway and to the London theater."

She nodded, considering his words. "I bet you've been to the ballet and the opera, too."

He nodded. "Can you dance?" he asked.

"I can, but I have a trick ankle that lands me flat on the ground sometimes," she confessed. "I don't want to risk that happening on stage."

"Did you hurt it in the circus?"

"No, I was born with it. It's just one of those weird things."

A chorus girl with a full mane of wild red curls, dressed in yellow tap pants and a short top, came toward them. "Del, Lenny is wanting you," she reported in heavily accented English.

"I'll be right there." Delilah looked up at Bert at an angle that suddenly made her seem very young to him. He realized she was still in her teens, which he hadn't thought before that moment. "See you tomorrow, okay?"

"Okay," he agreed as she hurried back toward her dressing room.

He noticed that the chorus girl who had come for Del was idling nearby, looking him up and down. "Want to buy a girl a late supper?" she asked flirtatiously.

He didn't really want to buy anyone anything until his check for this article came in, but she was cute and he was tired of eating alone. "Will you be wearing that outfit?" he asked her.

"If you like, I will."

"Sure, but you'll need a coat."

They went to a café he liked to frequent when he was in the Montmartre section of the city. It was simple but the food was great.

Her name was Yvette. It was easy to talk to her because she did most of the talking. She told him how she worked as a maid in a hotel until she had met Lenny there one day and he offered her a job at his club.

"How did he know you could dance?" Bert asked.

"I couldn't. I think he just liked me. It's better than being a maid." She continued talking, telling him about her life while also asking him about his. He got the feeling that she was trying to tease out the precise status of his finances and it was confusing her. "So your family is rich but you are not? How can that be?" she asked.

"Because I don't want to run my dad's dishware factory," he explained. "It seems like a form of slavery to me."

"It's not slavery when you are the son of the boss," she pointed out.

"It's not about the money," he disagreed.

"Everything is about money," she said offhandedly, picking at her escargot shell with a small fork. He blanched slightly, watching her; he could never get used to eating snails.

"I could sing her part, you know," Yvette said, drawing the snail from its shell with her fork. "You should interview me. Forget her."

"You don't like Miss Jones?" he asked.

"She's . . . how can I say it . . . stuck on herself. She is not so much. I can be like an Egyptian girl, too. I have the feel for it. But not with that big black cat. No."

"Well, when you have an act going, I'll come and interview you. Can you sing?"

"I can do anything," she said, wiping her mouth. "If they pay me, I can do it."

Three men entered the café. They wore the uniform of the Nazi Party. He had seen them while on a trip to Berlin and had instantly decided they were not for him. He despised their arrogance and had heard stories of terrible brutality. He had been handed pamphlets in the street and the anti-Jewish slander they contained had repulsed him.

They took a table nearby. When they ordered, they spoke in voices he found overly loud. They continued their conversation in German, which he didn't understand.

"Let's go," he told Yvette before she was quite finished. He was suddenly overwhelmed with fatigue and wanted nothing more than to sleep in the small furnished room he was renting.

He left Yvette at the theater and caught a cab back to his room. Once he was away from her and no longer listening to the Germans, his fatigue lifted a bit. He was even inspired to work on a new song idea. It was about a woman who walked a panther on a leash.

Someone knocked on his door and he grunted, annoyed at being disturbed from his song. It was probably the hotel owner looking for the weekly rent, which he now no longer had in its entirety because he'd treated Yvette to supper.

That was a dumb move, he chided himself, pulling open the door. He began to think of what he would say to persuade the hotel owner to wait.

But the man on the other side was not the hotel owner. He was tall and wore an overcoat. His expression was so dour that Bert instantly decided he was some sort of policeman.

"Robert Brody?" the man asked with a trace of an English accent.

Bert nodded.

"British Intelligence," the man said, producing an ID card from his wallet. "Might I come in to speak to you for a moment?"

Lenny left Del's dressing room and pulled a pack of cigarettes from his pocket. Tonight, when he tried to put his arms around her, she'd managed to slip out of his grasp, giggling and making a joke of it yet again.

Once more, he was leaving her dressing room frustrated and angry. Rubbing his jaw thoughtfully, he considered the situation. How much longer was he going to put up with this evasiveness from her? He wasn't sure.

What did she want from him? The girls were all crazy about him. And why shouldn't they be? Not yet twenty-five, he was the youngest club owner in Paris. With cash backing from some men he'd known back in Chicago, he'd opened The Panther and turned it into one of the hottest spots in Paris. It was a good thing, too, because his partners in Chicago were not the kind of men he would want to make unhappy.

When Del had walked in with that crazy big cat on a leash, he'd even named the club for her pet. He'd made her a headliner, hadn't he? He had bought the panther the emerald-studded collar, too. The jewels would have cost a fortune if his connections in Chicago hadn't hooked him up with a man in Paris who got things like that for a good price. He had staked everything he had on his gut intuition that she had what it took.

The time had come for Del to show him some gratitude.

It wasn't that he just wanted to be with her. There were plenty of chorus girls for that — flirty little Yvette, for one. She'd tumble for him in a second; she'd as much as told him so. Almost all the chorus girls would love to have him — but that wasn't all he was after.

Delilah Jones was the real thing: a little brassy around the edges, maybe, but that could be polished. She was the whole package: talent, looks, style — funny and smart. And more than that, most important of all, she had star quality. When Delilah Jones walked into a room, everyone noticed.

He could mold her into the biggest star Paris had ever seen ... but he wasn't going to waste his time doing it if she kept brushing him off like she'd been doing. He wanted them to be a team in every way possible.

"Hello, Lenny."

"Why are you still here, Yvette?" he asked, drawing on his cigarette.

"That reporter took me out to supper."

"Who? Bert Brody?" he asked with a contemptuous laugh. "You'll go out with anyone, won't you?"

"He's a nice boy, but he went home and I'm not tired. Maybe you will take me out to an after-hours club, yes?"

"Sure, why not?" he agreed, blowing out smoke.

The next day, Del hurried up the steep street leading to the Parthenon monument, one hand on the crochet hat that hugged her face and the other clutching her coat against the breeze.

She wanted this interview to go well but it was hard to keep her thoughts on it — not after what had happened last night. She had been home in her apartment cooking Baby's midnight snack — liver, very raw with sautéed onions, the way Baby liked it — when a strange man had come to her door. He was from British Intelligence, or so he had claimed. He asked her to work for them.

It seemed that a group of scientists were completing plans for a rocket that could, in theory, be launched from as far away as Berlin and would be able to accurately fire a missile on a target in London.

"But Germany is not at war with England," she'd pointed out.

"We have reason to think that could soon change," he'd replied.

They believed that the Nazi officers had been lingering in Paris, waiting to pick up the plans for this rocket and to pay the scientists. "They come into your club," he'd said. "We want you to circulate among them. Find out what you can learn."

"How will I contact you?"

"We'll contact you."

The dome of the Parthenon came into view. She wasn't sure why she'd selected it as a place to meet except that she'd always liked its roundness and columns. It seemed so stately and quiet, almost tomblike inside — so different from the boisterousness of the Left Bank, an oasis of calm. Some day she would like to see the original Parthenon in Greece. It had always appealed to her, was oddly homey. As she reached the top of the street leading into the traffic circle surrounding the Parthenon, she saw Bert Brody standing on the wide front steps in front of the monument.

He was the privileged American type she'd seen in magazines and sometimes glanced out at in an audience — college kids seeking a view of the seamier side of life before returning to the comfort of their own safe havens. She had never spoken to someone like him and she was eager to discover what he was like, as though he were some rare orchid she might never again have the opportunity to examine. If his attitude proved too condescending or superior, she had an exit strategy: She'd claim to be needed at the club. The important thing was not to lose her cool. He was writing an article about her act, after all. That gave him the final word.

From the far side of the traffic circle, she waved to him and he returned the gesture. Waiting for traffic to pass, she crossed to the Parthenon in the center. *"Bonjour,"* she greeted him brightly. *Show time*, she thought.

Together they re-crossed and she guided him to a small café she knew. Inside, they ordered and she began to fill him in on her background, the fictitious one that sprang to her mind — the nice Victorian home in Baltimore where she was raised by her proper aunts.

It was almost true.

She *had* lived in a nice home with her elderly grandmother until the woman had died when she was five. It was a dim memory and no doubt figured into her fantasy about the aunts. When she was eight, she'd walked out of the orphanage she was living in, preferring to take her chances on her own. No one had come looking for her.

"What did your aunts think about you joining the circus? Last night you said you had been in the circus," he reminded her.

"Umm . . . my aunts were not in favor of my theatrical ambitions, and as an artist I needed to stretch beyond the restrictions of the church choir."

"So you joined the circus?" he asked.

"Yes, but only on the weekends. During the week I had school and my operatic studies to attend to."

Was he buying this story?

She couldn't tell.

They talked through lunch and lingered long after she had insisted on paying the check. It surprised her that he had traveled on his own, working odd jobs and writing for newspapers and magazines to pay his way. He did not seem to possess the allowance from home that so many Americans abroad counted on. When she gently inquired about it, he told her that his father was stern and strong-minded. "If I wasn't going into his business, I was on my own. So here I am, penniless and free."

The assortment of odd jobs he'd worked almost equaled her list. He had even crewed on a sailing ship in Greece while writing a story for *Traveling Abroad* on the Grecian Parthenon. "Sailing is one of my great loves," he said.

"I've never been," she admitted. "Tell me more about Greece. How did you like it?"

He had loved it. She was intrigued by all he had to tell her. "Did you know that for a while instead of being the temple of Athena, the Greek Parthenon was dedicated to the Virgin Mary?" he told her.

"That's so interesting," she said sincerely. "They changed one strong, divine female figure for another. I wonder if throughout history, people just give different names to powers that are more or less the same."

"I've often thought the same thing," he said. "And we fight about differences which are really not so different if you scratch beneath the surface."

"I think so, too. It seems so obvious but people will get seriously upset at you if you say such a thing."

He sat back and studied Delilah as though he also was revising his idea of who she was. A waiter came by to light a candle in a votive on the table. Del covered it before the waiter reached the wick. "Please don't," she requested.

"*Mademoiselle* does not like the candle?" the waiter questioned.

"No, *s'il vous plaît.*"

The waiter nodded and moved on.

"I'm a little skittish around fire," Del explained to Bert. "I never liked it, but when Baby was a cub, I had to run into a burning tent and pull her from her cage." Throwing her head back, she laughed heartily. "I let all the big cats out. It was the only way I could save their lives. What a crazy scene that caused!"

He laughed, too. "It must have been wild!"

"Yes, but there was no choice: I couldn't let them die in there."

"I suppose that's when you moved on to vaudeville," he guessed.

"Yes," she said, still laughing at the memory. "The circus owners were not so happy with me after that. But do you know the funny thing? After that incident, I wasn't as afraid of fire anymore. All my life I had been terrified of it. I still don't like it, but it no longer gives me the screaming heebie-jeebies like it once did."

He pretended to write on his pad. "Delilah Jones has overcome her fear of fire by running into a burning building."

Hearing him speak those words struck a deep chord within her. What he said was true. She'd known it but had never stopped to take in how much she'd really accomplished by running into that burning tent.

Standing, she went to the counter and took a box of matches from a bowl. When she returned to the table, she struck a match. "To *completely* overcoming our fears," she said as she lit the candle.

"I'm all for it," Bert said, smiling. "Good for you."

"Thanks. It feels good."

"You're an interesting woman, Delilah," he said. "You were once nervous around candles but not man-eating big cats."

That made her chuckle. "Baby is a pussycat. I'm thinking of changing her name to something more theatrical like Cleopatra or Nefertiti but I'm worried it might confuse her."

"Delilah Jones is a pretty theatrical name," he remarked. "Is it your real name or a stage name?"

"I heard it in the Bible and liked it so I took it up when I joined the circus. I'll tell you my real name if you swear to keep it secret. If you put it in the article, I'll find you and murder you in your sleep."

"I swear."

"Louisa. Louisa Jones. My grandma, who had been a slave until after the Civil War, named me for an aunt of mine, her first child, who she never saw again after she was sold downriver. Later, someone told her that Louisa Jones had died fighting in the Civil War. She had pretended to be a man to enlist."

"Wow! What a gutsy woman!" he said. "My great-uncle John was a Union soldier. My great-uncle survived the war although he died sort of young anyway; he was in his fifties. After the war, he opened up a little pottery business and did so well that it eventually became May's Dishware."

"That's a giant huge business," she said, impressed. "It must be worth a bundle. I thought all you idle rich folks inherited money. I didn't know any of you actually earned it."

"My father and I didn't earn it. Great-uncle John earned the first money, and then the rest of the family inherited it," Bert admitted with a wry laugh. "Great-uncle John divorced his wife and never remarried, so my father inherited the dishware factories. That's the fate I'm trying to avoid right now."

"By writing?" she asked.

"Yes. I write articles, but my big love is writing songs. My dream is to somehow make a living at it."

"It's not such an impossible dream. Can I see some of your songs?"

"Sure, but they're in my hotel room. Want to come back there? I'll show them to you." Almost at the same moment the words came out of his mouth, he could feel the heat rising in his cheeks and cursed the fact that he blushed so easily. From the smile on her face, she had definitely noticed. "I know that just sounded like a cheap line," he quickly stammered. "I promise I'll behave."

"Don't make promises you can't keep," she replied, still grinning.

"Well, now I have no choice. I have to behave."

"Let's go," she replied, taking her coat from the back of the chair.

His room was on a shabby side street, but she felt at ease with him as they went up the steep, narrow stairs. Their lunch conversation had left her with the feeling that she knew him better than she actually did. "Occasionally you meet people you feel you've known all your life," she commented when she stepped into his room. Papers, books, and notebooks sat in loose piles on chairs, dressers, and on the one table.

"I know what you mean," he agreed.

"Is it happening now?" she dared to ask him.

He nodded slowly, gazing into her eyes. "I think so, yes," he murmured, as if falling into a dream.

Sure he was going to kiss her, she prepared to kiss him back, but after lingering a moment longer, he turned away. "Let me find those songs."

Her sting of disappointment gave way to admiration. No doubt he didn't want her to think he was taking advantage of the situation. He had class. And he had promised to behave.

She picked a hardcover book off the table and read its cover. "*Siddhartha* by Hermann Hesse — what's this about?"

"It's about the life of Buddha and his path to enlightenment," he replied, digging through the clutter of his papers. "It was written about fifteen years ago."

"Are you interested in Buddhism?"

"I like Hesse's writing and I've read some of his other books. But I don't know about this one. It feels a little predictable. I can always guess what will happen next even though I don't know much about Buddhism. It's strange."

He found his marble notebook of songs. "Here it is." Though he had no piano, he sang the songs for her and she quickly picked up the tunes, singing along. They were smooth together, seamlessly flowing with each other so that it was impossible to tell who was leading and who was following. They were simply effortlessly together.

"My voice never sounded better."

"My songs never sounded better."

They spoke at the same time, their voices overlapping, and then they laughed at the collision of their words. As their laughter drifted off, they continued to look into each other's eyes.

"These songs are great," she said after another moment, meaning it. "Would you really let me sing one of them in my act?"

"All of them, if you like. I never dreamed they could sound so wonderful until I just heard you sing them."

"They *are* wonderful," she agreed. "I especially like this one about the lovers who have just met feeling that they've met before. Did you write it about someone special?"

He shook his head. "No, it just came to me one day. Funny . . . I could have written it just today because that feeling is so strong." The red came into his cheeks again. "Not that we're together, of course."

"Of course," she echoed, though she now knew it was inevitable that they would be.

Another moment thick with possibility passed between them as they stood just a little too close together, neither one speaking. Longing to kiss him, she resolved not to make the first move forward.

"Could I come to the club tomorrow in the morning?" he asked, breaking the spell. "We could use the piano there to run through the songs."

"That's a swell idea," she said jauntily. "Be there at ten in the morning. Wait — make it twelve. I sleep late."

"Great. I'll walk you home."

"You don't have to."

"No. I want to."

"All right, then. I'm not going home, though. I have an appointment: It's sort of a doctor I've been seeing, a psychoanalyst."

"I've heard of Sigmund Freud. Like him?"

"Yeah." She gazed up at him, suddenly worried. "Don't mention that in your article. Promise?"

"Promise. Is something bothering you, if you don't mind my asking? Is it the fire thing?"

She shook her head. "Someday when I know you better, I'll tell you."

"Okay."

On the stairs, he held her arm to stop her descent to the first landing where the hotel owner was sweeping. "Wait 'til he goes, okay?" Bert whispered.

She smiled at him. "Can't pay?"

He nodded, reddening a bit once again. "Not yet."

"I know how it feels," she assured him. "Don't worry. You're going to be famous soon. We both are." Reaching into her purse, she took out some bills. "Want a down payment on your songs?"

"Thanks. I'll wait," he declined.

"For what?"

He smiled. "Pay me when you make your first recording of the songs."

This was not fake; Delilah could tell he meant every word. "Do you really think I could make a record?" she asked.

"You've got the talent. Now you've got the songs. All you need is the right break," he replied confidently. "It'll come."

The very idea of her own record made her sigh with longing. "Wouldn't that be wonderful?"

At three the next afternoon, Bert hurried up the steps to his hotel room sure of one thing: He was in love with Delilah Jones.

They'd worked together since noon down at the club. He played the piano while she sang each of his songs. If he'd ever believed the songs were good, now he was positive.

Her voice made every word take on a deeper meaning. He couldn't imagine how such a young woman could breathe so much worldly suffering and poignancy into each phrase. The things she must have been through and seen to bring so much depth to her performance. It was a long way from Isis, the nicest on the Nile.

Hearing her today made him explode with love and longing for her.

He hadn't kissed her because he hadn't wanted to cause gossip there at the club. Lenny was lurking, making excuses to pass by, commenting that he wasn't sure the songs were right for the club. Del had told him to be open-minded.

Finally, at two-thirty, Lenny had told them they had to

go. He needed the stage so the chorus girls could rehearse a new number.

"Let me keep these," she'd said, gathering up the songs. "I'll go over them myself and then rehearse them with Al, our pianist."

"Okay. See you tonight," he said, taking hold of her hand. "I know you'll be great."

"If I am, it will be because of these songs," she replied. "They're beautiful."

"You're beautiful."

Just then, the chorus girls came clacking onto the stage and Al the pianist, a thin black man, came in to claim his piano. Letting go of her hand, Bert left ... even though he keenly wanted to stay.

Coming into his room, he threw himself onto the threadbare loveseat. He closed his eyes in order to conjure the image of her face, to hear again the honey tones of her voice.

She had his songs. Maybe she was singing them right now. Was she thinking of him as he was imagining her? He hoped so.

Tonight after the show, after she debuted his songs, he would tell her how he felt. He'd find the right moment to kiss her. He was pretty sure from the way she gazed into his eyes as she sang that she felt the same about him.

That night, Del had tears of happiness in her eyes as the people in the club jumped to their feet, applauding. They'd cheered for her before, but this was different. There was no stomping or whistling, like when she did her comic material. She had moved these people by singing Bert's songs. Some of the women were crying with abandon.

Standing at the piano with Baby seated in front of her, she presented Al to the audience, encouraging them to give him his share of the applause. She saw Bert out in the audience and waved for him to come forward. He shook his head.

"Thank you so much, ladies and gentlemen," she said, quickly wiping her eyes. "You are so kind. The genius who wrote these great new songs is in the audience tonight. Please give a hand to a brilliant songwriter, Bert Brody." She signaled the man who ran the spotlight to direct it at Bert.

Caught in the round circle of light, Bert waved sheepishly to the applauding audience.

Later, when everyone had finally left, she changed her clothes, leashed Baby, and came out again to the front of the club. Bert was waiting for her, sitting alone at a table. He stood when he noticed her.

There was nothing she could think of to say to him. He'd said it all in his songs and she'd echoed it back to him. When she reached his table, he put his arms around her and drew her close.

Reaching around his neck, she fell into his embrace, kissing him. Something within her opened and let the energy of this kiss, this contact, flow through her. It felt strange and new and familiar and safe all at once.

At that moment, she knew that she loved him.

Three weeks later, Bert was whistling as he came up the stairs. There was no more need to skulk into his room, avoiding the hotel owner. Lenny had doubled Del's salary since the club was packed night after night. Del had insisted on giving him a cut of it for his songs.

They'd spent every night since then having late suppers and taking moonlit strolls along the Seine, basking in the joy of their new love. In the afternoons, when she wasn't seeing her psychoanalyst, they worked on new material. Sometimes he read to her, mostly love poems.

When he unlocked his door, he found the man from British Intelligence seated in the red velvet chair by the one window overlooking the street. "How did you get in?" he demanded to know.

"It's not important," the Intelligence man replied. "I didn't want to loiter outside; it attracts attention." He opened a briefcase to reveal British pounds, neatly bundled. In these past weeks at the club, he'd heard bits and pieces of suspicious conversation that he'd mentioned when this man came by to check. It hadn't seemed very important to Bert, but the man assured him that anything might be important.

"Tonight you'll give this money to your contact. She

will pass you the rocket blueprints." Bert had been told about these prints days earlier. He hadn't known there would be an exchange tonight. "Your contact will pay the scientists who gave the prints to her. You don't want to be responsible for what happens if she doesn't get this money."

"How will I recognize my contact?"

"Go to The Panther tonight. An agent will slip you a note telling you how to recognize her."

"Can't you just tell me who it is?"

The Intelligence man left the case behind as he headed for the door. "The less you know, the better. The agent can't do it for you because he might be recognized." At the door, he turned back. "And don't skim from that case, not even a little. The whole amount has to be delivered."

Bert would do this just as he'd been requested to. England and America were allies, so he felt it was his patriotic duty. And the Nazis had repulsed him. In no way could they be allowed to gain the military superiority this rocket might provide them. Nazis in England — the thought made him shudder.

Dr. LeFleur peered at Del through his thick glasses. Lines of vivid orange sunset striped the small darkened room despite the fact that the elderly doctor had drawn the blinds to block it. Below, Del was dimly aware of the rumble of evening traffic like the crash of a river steadily tumbling over rocks.

She enjoyed seeing Dr. LeFleur once a week, but so far he'd done nothing to quiet the terrifying dreams that plagued her sleep. She'd had them since childhood, but lately they were growing worse. She would wake up shrieking, helpless. She became so hysterical that a few of the neighbors had even petitioned the landlord to evict her. The only reason he hadn't was that she got home from the club so late and these fits occurred in the morning when most of the other tenants were working.

"Tell me, what are you feeling now?" the analyst prompted gently. "Let's see if we can't get to the heart of these troubling dreams."

Del shifted a bit on the green leather couch and closed her eyes. "It's funny," she said. "This room reminds me of a cave I dreamed about last night, though I've never been in a cave."

"Picture the cave. What else is in it?" he asked.

"There is a woman in there with me. She is my mother, but maybe not . . . she's someone's mother."

"You do not recall your actual mother, true?"

"That's right. She left me with my grandmother when I was an infant. My grandmother was wonderful, but she died when I was small."

"Perhaps you seek a strong mother figure in your dreams who can take her place."

"Maybe. In the dream she's telling me something, but I don't understand what she means." Opening her eyes,

Delilah turned to him. "Where are these pictures coming from, Dr. LeFleur?"

"They arise from deep in your unconscious mind. Over these weeks that we have been talking, I see that you are a young woman who is in unusually keen contact with your unconscious; many creative people are. These images may be manifestations of your greatest fears and desires. You may be calling forth symbols that are universal to all people but are manifest in different ways. Or there is another possibility."

"What is that?" she asked.

"It is possible that these are memories."

"Memories? But I told you I've never been in a cave. I dream all sorts of things that can't be real."

"I would like to try something with you today. It's called a hypnotic regression. It might help you to remember a past life."

"What past life?" she asked.

"On my most recent trip to America, I learned of a man named Edward Cayce. He falls asleep and claims he has dream visions of a person's past lives. I witnessed one of these readings and was most impressed."

"Could you read my past lives?" Del asked.

"No. I don't have that gift. But I studied the methods of hypnotism set down by Milton Erickson and even met the man on my trip. Would you mind if I hypnotized you?"

"I suppose not."

"Good. Close your eyes once again. Now relax. Count backward from ten. Good. You are feeling sleepy, very sleepy. . . ."

Eyes narrowed for focus, Lenny released the dart from his hand. It flew straight and swift to the dartboard on his office wall. Bull's-eye! Again. He was so good at this, it was getting boring. But darts soothed his nerves and helped him think.

Two problems weighed on him at the moment.

He had to get rid of this Brody character. He hated him, pure and simple. Once he was gone, Lenny could win back Del's affections. But as long as Brody hung around, Del had eyes only for him.

Now, a way to do this had presented itself. The phone call he'd just received had come at the perfect time.

He went to the office doorway, gazing into the halls where chorus girls, musicians, and stagehands were preparing for the night's performance. "Yvette," he called when he spotted her, trailing her yellow feathered boa behind her tap outfit. "A word, please."

She clacked toward him in her tap shoes, tilting her head like an alert canary. "*Oui?*"

"Come inside." Offering her a seat, he sat behind his desk. Tilting his chair back casually, he made her a proposition. For a large amount of francs, would she be willing to be very friendly with Bert Brody tonight? Perhaps she would want to take him up onto the roof with her?

"I'll show him the lights of Paris," she said with a laugh. "Why do you want me to do this?"

"I want Del to forget him," he divulged, although it was only part of the truth, "and to see he can't be trusted."

"What if she *can* trust him?"

"He took you to dinner, didn't he? He's attracted to you, even if you don't appeal to his better nature."

"I can get him up there and then throw myself into his arms when Del shows up. One way or another, I'll make it work. I have a condition, though. I'll do it if you make me the headliner of the show." Yvette fancied herself to be a shrewd negotiator.

"I can't do that; Del's my hot draw. She wants a night off, though. What if I give it to her on Sunday and you headline that night?"

"Sunday? The place is empty on Sunday."

He shrugged. "It's the best I can do."

"Okay," she agreed. "Sunday — I headline *and* I get the money?"

"And the money," he assured her.

"Tonight?" she checked.

"Tonight."

"All right." Tossing her curls behind her shoulders, she grinned at him. "Nice doing business with you."

Rocking forward in his chair, Lenny rubbed his jaw. He'd make sure Del caught Bert Brody in a compromising position with Yvette. And this solved his second concern as well. One of his backers in Chicago, a German immigrant businessman, had a brother back in Berlin, a Nazi officer. The businessman had referred his Nazi brother to Lenny as a man who could be trusted to accomplish whatever was asked of him. That officer had just phoned him, revealing that Bert Brody was working for British Intelligence. "We are told he comes to your club every night. Tonight he will be delivering money for the British. It's in a case he will have. Don't let him make that delivery."

Tonight he would bring Del to the roof. She would find Bert with Yvette. Lenny would provoke a fight with him. In the skirmish, he'd go off the roof. Lenny would get the case from him and take some of the money for himself before turning it over to the Nazis.

He went to his safe and turned the tumbler until it opened. He took out his handgun and shoulder holster. If anything went wrong, he'd rely on this.

Bert arrived early to The Panther. He couldn't wait to turn over this suitcase of money. It filled him with anxiety. It seemed so obvious that he was carrying money, as though the case itself had a glowing dollar sign on it. What if he was robbed? How would he explain *that*?

Why hadn't they selected a tough guy, someone more

formidable — a boxer, maybe? The only two sports he was good at were sailing and archery. Despite his nerves, his lip quirked into a grin as he imagined strolling the streets of Paris with bow and arrow slung over his arm. Ridiculous as it would appear, it would be some protection at least.

He walked into the empty club. A janitor in front was removing the chairs that had been stacked on the tables. Otherwise the place was empty.

In a half hour, the show was scheduled to start. There would be a few acts with the chorus girls, a comedian, another chorus girl act, and then Delilah would appear and remain onstage for the rest of the act.

He took a stacked chair off a table and sat, placing the case at his side. He kept his right hand on top of it, not losing contact with it for a second.

Yvette walked out from the wings of the stage and down center. "Bert, I need to speak to you," she said, swinging her legs over the side and dropping her feet to the floor. He stayed seated, not wanting the case to be conspicuous. "Del saw you come in. She sent me with a message. She wants you to meet her on the roof. It's very important."

He couldn't leave, not until the agent gave him the information that would identify his contact. "Would you tell her I might be a little while?" he asked.

"What are you waiting for?"

"It's nothing. If you'd tell her I'll be along, I'd appreciate it a great deal."

"It will cost you another supper."

"Please."

"I'll tell her. The door to the roof is backstage to the right, up the stairs behind the first door you come to. I'll make sure it's unlocked." Her message relayed, Yvette sauntered off the stage, into the wings.

Maybe he had better go outside, he considered. The agent might be waiting there. Now he was anxious to know what Del wanted, eager to pass on the briefcase and be done with this espionage.

He got up to go when, glancing down, he noticed a folded paper on the table in front of him.

It hadn't been there before! He was sure of it.

Checking around, he saw no one. The only change in the club was that the janitor had finished his work and left.

The janitor. Of course!

He unfolded the paper. The note read: EMERALD COLLAR.

He imagined a lavishly dressed woman with an emerald choker around her neck. Then he remembered: Baby wore an emerald-studded collar.

Del was his contact!

Del scratched Baby behind the ears with her short red fingernails. She held her leash tightly as they paced the alley behind the club. Del was nervous and Baby always picked up on her emotions with an uncanny sympathy.

She had no idea who her contact would be. The man from British Intelligence had assured her it was for the best. A man would approach her with a briefcase filled with money. She had picked up the rocket plans already from a man who had come to her apartment that evening. He would return that night for the money. He warned her that if she didn't have it, he would kill her.

Lenny came out into the alley. "Shouldn't you be getting ready to go onstage?" he asked.

She opened her coat to reveal her red dress. "I'm ready."

"Good. Come up to the roof with me for a moment. There's something there I think you should see."

"What?"

"You'll see."

She didn't have time for this, but what if Lenny was the person who was going to hand her the cash? He was an American, after all — he could be the one. "All right," she agreed, following him inside.

Locking Baby in her dressing room, she went with Lenny up the stairs to the roof.

On the other side of the door to the roof, someone was arguing, though she couldn't tell what was being said. What was this all about? Impulsively, she unlatched the bolt and pushed the door open. Yvette and Bert were facing each other.

Yvette sprang to his side, clutching his arm. "You told me she would never find out about us!" she cried.

"What are you talking about?" Bert replied angrily. He turned to Del. "Yvette said to meet you on the roof. You weren't here so I was about to leave but the door got locked from the inside."

"How can you lie like that?" Yvette accused him. "You brought me up here so we could be alone. That's what you told me."

"Why are *you* lying?" Bert shot back. "You told me Del was up here."

With darting eyes, Del saw the briefcase in his hand. With an almost imperceptible glance at her, he confirmed that he was the one she had to contact.

Whatever was going on, the important thing was that she get that case and give him the plans. This other business could be sorted out later. She was sure it was some sort of trick. Lenny had probably put Yvette up to it. He was jealous as anything these days.

"It's all right," Del said coolly. "Bert and I just met. It's not like he owes me an explanation. He can fool around with you all he wants, for all I care."

Turning to go back inside, she came face to face with a man stepping through the rooftop door. Another man came through the door behind the first man and he had a gun in his hands.

"What's this?" Yvette yelled at the men. "Put that gun away."

With a deafening explosion of sound, he shot her in the shoulder, throwing her back against a smoke stack. Sobbing in pain, she clutched her shoulder and passed out. Del couldn't tell if she was dead or alive.

The first man spoke in a heavy German accent. "We've intercepted the traitors who gave you the plans. They are dead now. Unless you want to be dead also, please give me the plans."

He aimed his gun at Del as she hopped onto the wall surrounding the roof. She knew there was a fire escape right below them.

The man fired at her.

Lenny leaped at the man as the shot was fired, shielding Del with his body. The bullet threw him back before dropping him hard onto the black tar roof.

The German agent fired again. He missed Del but her ankle turned beneath her. She was going over.

Flailing wildly, she fell backward, and the world swirled around her as she tumbled off the roof. Reaching out desperately, she grabbed hold of the outside railing of the fire escape, screaming as her arm wrenched in its socket and her head snapped back. Her high heels clattered down, bouncing off the metal stairs as her legs kicked out, dangling in the air.

Looking up, she saw Bert coming over the roof toward her.

Another shot rang out and he sailed off the roof wall, his briefcase opening midair, money swirling around him, whirling through the night.

Two more shots.

OhGodOhGod! He flew past her. She swung out and nearly caught hold of his sleeve but he slipped past her fingers.

NoNoNoNoNo!!!! Turning her head away, she heard him hit the ground.

"Help!" she shouted, swinging there by one arm. "Somebody help him! HELP!"

No one came. She had to help him.

Her heart pounding wildly, Del managed to get her second hand positioned on one of the railings. Kicking hard, she tried to get a foothold on the fire escape, but couldn't manage it.

Someone was clanging down the metal stairs toward her. Terrified, she glanced up sharply.

"Hang on." Lenny grabbed her by her wrists and lifted her onto the staircase. His white shirt was covered in blood.

"We have to help Bert," she sobbed, starting to climb down.

"I don't think it will matter," Lenny replied.

Then

I stand in the alley and look down at my money-covered body. Blood is making an ever-widening pool under my head. Nasty. I turn away but then must look back, fascinated by my own shattered self.

Del is climbing down to me, and Lenny follows her. Then she is sitting in the alley beside my lifeless body, shaking me. "Bert! Wake up! Wake up!" she screams. "Bert!"

She's in hysterics.

Lenny kneels beside her, puts his arm around her consolingly.

The next thing I see is hard to watch. She leans her head on his chest and sobs — cries and cries like her heart has cracked open and every sorrow is spilling out.

I had known she loved me. Now I realize how much.

I have to give Lenny credit; although blood was gushing out of his shoulder, he just sat there rubbing her back. That's one of the crazy things about people: They keep fooling you.

Nobody shoots down at us or comes over the wall. I guess Lenny has shot the enemy agents. His gun is holstered at his side. Rising again, I decide to go to the roof and see what happened.

Sure enough, the two Germans lie dead. The velvet bag with the plans is not there and neither is Yvette. It isn't hard to trace her, though, because there is a trail of blood going down the stairs.

Down in the club, no one seems to know what has happened yet, but the stage manager is looking for Del because she is supposed to go on soon. I find Yvette in a dark corner leaning heavily on the man from British Intelligence. She is handing him the plans for the rocket.

Well, what do you know — scrappy, cunning, self-serving Yvette is working for British Intelligence. I follow them outside and watch while the Intelligence guy gets into a cab with her. Together, they drive off. I hope he's taking her to a hospital.

Okay, she did try to seduce me and possibly get me killed, but I have to admire her spunk. When you're already dead, these things don't seem to matter as much. You can take the larger view.

And I am dead.

At that moment, it really hits me.

D-E-A-D . . . as a doornail, an expression that never made any sense to me.

This gives me a unique perspective. I could write a song about being dead from the stance of someone who really knows.

But I guess that's the point of being dead — one of them, anyway. You can't . . . write a song or anything else. Because you're dead.

I go back down to the alley. Del is still there, draped over my body. Sobbing.

Lenny has moved against the wall. He's pale. I guess the blood loss is getting to him.

"Hey, Del," I say gently. "Don't cry. I'm right here. I'll stay with you."

She looks up as though she's heard me and she reaches out like a kid groping in the dark for a light switch. Her hand passes right through me.

"Bert," she whispers. "Bert?"

I try to take her hand. Now it's my hand that passes through.

I'm no help to her this way. What good will it do if I stay with her? It will only keep her from loving someone who is alive. It wouldn't be fair. She's already had such a tough life. She doesn't deserve to be alone.

"Good-bye, Del," I say, trying to brush back some hair that's fallen in front of her eyes. "I love you."

"I love you, Bert," she whispers, as though somehow she's heard me.

I'm not sure where to go after that. Then, like an answer to that question, a gigantic white angel appears at the far end of the alley.

It reaches out a hand and beckons for me to come toward it.

And then in the next second I wonder if it is an angel. It might be a column of light.

Either way, I know what it wants.

I shake my head and back away. Not me. I'm not leaving.

I'm too attached to this life to think of going into that light.

I turn my back and walk away.

It's official, I think. *I'm a ghost.*

In the next weeks, months, years — it's very hard to keep track when you're a ghost — I roam around. The things I see would fill a book. For a while, I narrate some of what I see to a writer. He thinks the ideas are his, of course. His books sell well. I even manage to write some more songs, sitting beside a well-known lyricist as he struggles, whispering inspiration into his ear.

I want to stay because the world is too beautiful to abandon. What I am seeing, though, is less and less beautiful by the day. War and more war, death, starvation. Misery of every description.

I see Jews and others rounded up and taken to the obscene camps, crammed into cattle cars without food or water for days. I stay on the trains. I try to be comforting; sing to the children; recite poetry to the old people.

I see other ghosts doing the same thing.

I see angels. Many angels.

One day in 1942, Yvette is herded onto a train headed for the Dancy Deportation Center just north of Paris. From there, she and the others will be transported to one of the larger camps: Auschwitz, Dachau, Treblinka.

She is older but still pretty. Her red curls are cut to her chin. She wears a beret and a navy blue coat with the collar turned high. I sit beside her. "Don't be frightened. I'll stay with you," I say. She is someone I knew, after all.

She looks up sharply. She's heard me. "Are you an angel?" she whispers.

"Yes," I lie. It seems a more comforting reply; my being a ghost might frighten her.

Yvette sits on the floor, her arms wrapped around her knees. I sit beside her. As she speaks in a soft whisper, people glance at her as though she is insane. It seems that no one else can hear me. She notices the glances but doesn't care. Besides, under the circumstances, who would blame her if she's become unstrung?

"Have you seen Del?" I can't resist asking. Through all my ghostly roaming I never forget our love, though I resist the urge to check up on her. Thinking of what might have been is too painful.

"I saw her once in a while. We both spied for the French Underground."

"You're a hero," I comment, recalling how she had turned the rocket plans over to the British.

"Not really. You know," she says, "in many ways I have always been a treacherous girl. It seemed stupid to care about anyone other than myself. Taking care of me was such a huge job as it was. I have never thought of myself as a good person. But this situation is too atrocious for even me to bear. I've helped some people these last few years. If I die now, I can go knowing my life hasn't been wasted. I've never felt that before."

She is not the same Yvette I took to dinner. The war has changed her — for the better.

I squeeze her hand. I don't know if she feels it. "We're all on a journey," I say, realizing for the first time that this is true.

Before Dancy, the train stops in a field. I look at all the victims of the Nazi Gestapo, all doomed to unthinkable fates.

I am seized with a burning desire to do something for these people. I am a ghost, a rebel defying the laws of the universe. I can intervene, change destiny.

Why have I never realized it before?

With that thought, I pass through the train wall, unlock the door, and try to throw it open. It stays shut. I lack the physical solidity for the task.

Then, later that night, the train strikes something and comes undone. The door is rattled right off its hinges and the people inside push. What a satisfying thud as it crashes, falling out onto the field.

The people pour from the train, scrambling down the sloped field.

"Go!" I shout to Yvette but she isn't paying attention. A boy of about four is afraid to jump from the train. His mother is frantically waiting below while Yvette passes him down.

A Gestapo agent runs into the car, pistol raised. Yvette is the only one standing in the doorway and he shoots her immediately.

She leaps from her body before she even hits the ground.

"Bert! What are you doing here? I thought you were dead," she cries.

"I am, and so are you."

"No, I'm not. Come on." She tries to hurry children along, putting their hands into the hands of their fleeing parents. She tries to trip the Gestapo agents as they fire on the people in the field.

"That bullet went right through me. Did you see it?" she asks me, gleefully looking at her slim waist in shock. "I should be dead."

"You are dead."

"You're crazy. How could I be dead? That was lucky."

Many dead are appearing — more and more of them

by the moment. They are helping Yvette try to assist the fleeing people. She is getting almost giddy with her new-found invulnerability as bullet after bullet passes through her. "They must be shooting blanks," she decides.

The dead suddenly stand stock still in the field. A towering column of light appears. Its hum is the dark call of a reverberating violin string. They begin moving toward the calling column.

"Look. The Eiffel Tower," Yvette says to me, pointing.

"Yvette, it's not the Eiffel Tower. Go toward it," I tell her urgently. "Don't waste time."

The world that is to come might be a horrendous thing. Most likely it will be. I don't want to think of her as a ghost roaming within the torture chambers of this new world.

Fear clouds her face and she backs away. "No, I'm frightened. No."

I don't want to be in this world any longer, either.

I take her hand. "We'll go together. Trust me. It will be better."

"All right. I trust you," she says, nodding.

Together we step into the column of light.

And the blessed process of forgetting begins.

Mississippi, 1964

Mike Rogers came to a three-way crossroads and stopped the car. One of the three girls in the back-seat leaned forward to push down the lock button next to him. "Roll up your window," she reminded him.

"It's too hot," Mike objected. The car's fan had conked out somewhere around Kentucky.

"The handbook says to," she insisted. "We should have done it miles ago, but I was just now leafing through the book and remembered."

Beside him, his older brother Ray snorted disdainfully. "I'm not roasting to death in this car. We're not in the Soviet Union. Don't be so paranoid."

"Shut up, Ray," Mike said, mildly annoyed (as he often was around Ray). "You didn't even come to the training in Ohio."

Ray rubbed his jaw, a habit that majorly irritated Mike. Whenever he did it, Mike could be fairly sure he was about to say something especially jerky. "I didn't come to your stupid training because I'd never have come on this lame-brain trip in the first place except Mom begged me to catch up with you and make sure you don't get your-self killed."

This was about the hundredth time he'd reminded Mike about this, implying that Mike was incapable of going it alone. It was not a gesture Mike appreciated. Most likely, Ray's true motivation for coming along was because he saw it as a treasure trove of available young women. Every time he turned around to the three in the backseat, he flashed that bright shark's smile at each of them. It made Mike want to kill him.

Ray had showed up on the last day of their training at the Western College for Women in Ohio. It had been organized by the Student Nonviolent Coordinating Committee, which the students referred to as "Snick." Ray had been warmly welcomed, as they all had been, but Ray was particularly welcome because he looked like the star football quarterback that he had been in college until graduating last year. A big, good-looking, All-American like Ray could come in handy if things got ugly — and they already had. Three Civil Rights volunteers had been murdered in just the first ten days of their drive to register Negro voters here in Mississippi. Two were white, one black. In addition, there had been beatings, arrests, and bombings.

Rolling up his window, Mike looked at the three signs at the crossroads: Savage, Alligator, Coldwater. One of the girls in the backseat had taken out a map. "We're headed for Ruleville, so I think we should go that way," she said, pointing.

"Isn't that where they beat up Fannie Lou Hamer just for registering to vote?" another girl asked.

"I think so," said the third. "Can you imagine?"

They drove down a two-lane road past sagging shacks made of wood and tar paper. Vistas of endless cotton fields spread out on both sides. In most cases, the cotton grew right to the front doors of the shacks. "Remember, go five miles under the speed limit," the first girl coached from the backseat.

"Is that from your handbook, too?" Ray asked disdainfully.

"Yes," she replied. "We don't want to give the local law enforcement any reason to arrest us."

"Paranoid," Ray muttered.

They stopped at the address they'd been given, just outside Ruleville. It was a simple, run-down, wooden house with an open front porch. Three other cars were parked in front. A man with a beard, wearing jeans, sandals, and a T-shirt with SNCC on it, came down the porch to greet them.

"Welcome, I'm Dave," he greeted as Mike rolled down his window. "There's a pot of chili inside and ice-cold soda."

"Hallelujah!" one of the girls cheered, stepping from the backseat and smoothing her madras shift dress. She led them up the steps, where they were met by other volunteers.

Mike stopped on the porch to bask in the cool of an old electric fan balanced precariously on a rickety table. Next to the fan was an open record player. At least the place had electricity. That was something.

Inside were twelve other volunteers — five guys and seven young women. All of them were college-age, white, with middle-class ways. They greeted Mike and his carload with smiles and offers of food and drink. Although his fellow idealists were all strangers, Mike felt right at home.

The house was dominated by one large central room, which contained a small, antiquated kitchen, a table with a linoleum top, and a faded green velvet couch. Two small bedrooms were behind this room.

After eating, the tall bearded man took out his guitar and led some singing. Perched on the table and the couch or cross-legged on the floor, they sang protest songs: "Eyes on the Prize," "Oh, Freedom," "Blowin' in the Wind," "We Shall Overcome."

Inspired by his hero, Bob Dylan, Mike had written three protest songs of his own. They were in the trunk of his car, and for a moment he entertained the idea of showing them to the group. But before he could work up the nerve, they moved on to popular songs like "I Want to Hold Your Hand" by the Beatles and "Chapel of Love" by the Dixie Cups. Ray grinned at the three girls from the backseat when they got up and did a rendition of "Leader of the Pack." Mike guessed Ray assumed they were thinking about him as they sang, "That's why I fell for . . . the leader of the pack."

"Tomorrow you'll start going door to door to register

voters," Dave told them at about ten o'clock. "It's not going to be easy. These people have already been threatened not to register and they know all too well that these are not idle threats. They won't trust you right away. You're white. Why should they? We have to be up early to avoid the worst of this heat. Better get some sleep."

"Should we lock the front door?" the handbook girl asked. During their training sessions in Ohio they had been instructed not to let themselves be taken by surprise at night. Makeshift headquarters like this one had already been set afire, bombed, or raided.

Dave shook his head. "It hasn't got a lock. Besides, we'll die of heat in here if we shut the inside door. Maybe one of us should stay awake. We'll change shifts every two hours."

"I'm not tired," Mike volunteered. He spread out his sleeping bag on the floor of the main room where the guys were sleeping and settled down with his hands behind his head. In minutes, he heard Ray's unmistakable snore, followed by Dave's sputtering version.

Silver moonlight rimmed everything as it flooded in through the screen door and kitchen window. It was still brutally hot. The crickets were nearly deafening and a mosquito had gotten into the room. When its shrill buzz stopped, he knew someone would feel the red circle of sting in the morning.

Afraid he might sleep, he walked out onto the porch, where the crickets were louder still. The fan was still on and he indulged himself again in its breeze before heading down to his car.

Inside his trunk was a knapsack of clothing sitting beside his unstrung bow and quiver of arrows, which he'd left there after his last competition. As usual, he'd won first place. Though not the super athlete Ray was, at least there was one shelf in their paneled den for his many archery awards.

From inside his knapsack he took out his paperback copies of Hermann Hesse's *Siddhartha* and Jack Kerouac's *The Dharma Bums*. Everyone he knew was reading Kerouac's *On the Road*. He found he preferred *The Dharma Bums*. He'd done some research and learned that dharma was an important concept in Hindu and Buddhist religions. It meant one's spiritual place in the universe, or what a person must do in order to do his spiritual duty.

Lately there was a lot of interest in eastern religions. *Siddhartha* was about Buddha's journey to become . . . well, Buddha. Buddhism interested Mike but he wasn't sure he quite understood it. It seemed to him it might take a lifetime to fully get it right.

Mike liked to think — or hoped, at least — that coming here to Mississippi was part of his spiritual duty.

Everything was up for grabs these days. Dylan's latest album said it all: *The Times They Are A-Changin'*. At least he hoped they were. He had come all this way to Mississippi to be part of that change. It might improve his karma — or maybe it was his dharma. He wasn't sure, but he was hopeful.

He sat on the porch, thinking these things, letting the fan wash over him. Remembering why he was awake, he stood and walked to the edge of the porch, scanning the miles of cotton fields for any sign of movement. He offered silent thanks to the moon for giving them such a well-lit night.

Turning back to the chair, he noticed again the beat-up record player on the table. The record on it was as worn and old looking as the player, but was probably even older. His grandmother had owned records like it. It was a collection of songs by a female singer he'd never heard of. Delilah Jones.

Curious, he turned it on, quickly lowering the volume so he wouldn't wake anyone. Immediately a bluesy jazz voice filled the night, singing of a lover who got away.

Slowly he sat, transfixed by the soaring voice that cut through time and space to reach him as nothing else had ever reached him before.

Louisa Raymond sat on the porch of the same house she'd lived in as a very young child, rocking and fanning herself. The young man walking up the dirt path to the house had parked down on the road. Squinting into the sunlight, she tried to see him more clearly. Lately things had become a bit blurrier than they'd once been, though in her estimate forty-seven was far from old. She was sure others, especially young people, would disagree. Fishing in the pocket of her cotton dress, she pulled out cat's-eye-shaped spectacles and held them to her eyes.

Right away, she knew his business.

He was one of those voter registration kids from up North. It was written all over him: the plaid cotton shirt, the slightly longish hair, the clipboard, and the way he moved, so crisp and alert.

"Good morning, ma'am," he addressed her with one foot on her bottom step. "I'm Mike Rogers. I was wondering: Are you registered to vote?"

"No, young man, I am not registered nor do I wish to be," she replied.

"Would it be all right if I asked why not?" he said politely.

She smiled slightly. These young volunteers had such a cordial way of talking. She admired that. Someone had coached these kids well. "Yes, you may ask. I do not wish to register to vote because there's trouble enough in this world without provoking it."

"What about your rights as an American?" he asked.

"As a *what*?" she asked, her voice rising into a hoot of derisive laughter.

The young man didn't smile. "You are an American, aren't you?"

"I suppose I am, but I have always considered myself

a citizen of the world. It's here in the United States that I must endure the indignities of second-class citizenship."

"And doesn't that make you angry?" he prodded.

"Where do you go to school, young man?" she countered, preparing to point out the great cultural gulf that divided them, how clueless he was about her life and what it was like. "Do you spend your weekends singing 'All Hail Harvard' or 'Yippee for Yale'?"

"I attend Princeton," he replied.

"So it's 'Pip! Pip! Princeton,' then."

As she spoke, the world tilted, actually seemed to lurch to one side. She gripped the sides of the chair to keep her balance.

In a bound, he was beside her. "Ma'am, are you all right? Can I get you anything?"

"Would you get me some water from inside?" she requested. "There are clean glasses in the dish drain."

Licking her lips, she scowled across the sun-bright fields. *What was that?* she asked herself. It might have been some new manifestation of the cancer in her breast, but she didn't think so. It felt like something else. Yes, it was something else and she realized what it was in a sudden flash of understanding.

Mike Rogers returned quickly with a glass of water. "Is it the heat?" he asked, crouching to hand it to her.

As she sipped the water she studied his hazel eyes and brown curly hair. "Have I met you before?" she asked.

"I don't believe so. I'm not from around here."

"I just experienced the most overwhelming déjà vu. Do you know that expression?"

"You felt that you'd lived through the exact same moment before?" he offered.

"Yes — just back when we were talking about Princeton. It was amazing."

His eyes grew larger. "I felt it, too."

Was he making fun of her?

He continued. "When you spoke those words, a picture came into my head. You were saying the same thing to me. You had a big black cat with you. Weird, huh?"

Louisa grabbed the walking cane hung at the side of her chair and stood abruptly. This time the world spun once, then twice. She gripped his arm as it spun again.

And then everything went black.

He laid the woman on the couch in her living room. He wasn't sure if this was the right thing to do, but he couldn't leave her outside in the heat. Hurrying back to the kitchen, he found a clean dishcloth, soaked it in cold water, and returned to the living room to lay it on her forehead.

It would probably be best if he just left, but that didn't seem like the right thing to do, either. What if she didn't come back to consciousness? He should call a doctor but he didn't know who to call. He'd give it another minute.

This was the nicest house he'd seen since arriving here, at least of those belonging to the blacks. It was solidly built with polished wood floors. Amber shades kept out the blistering sun, giving the place a golden glow. It was interestingly furnished, too, with pieces from several recent decades and others that had to be antiques.

One glassed-in china cabinet was filled with exquisite pottery: modern pieces like a hand-blown glass vase in swirling colors and a large plate with a Picasso print at its center; an ancient-looking Greek urn, and a whiskey flask from the Civil War era; there was even a blue stone hippo that looked like it was from Egypt.

He spotted a hardcover book on the table: *Their Eyes Were Watching God* by Zora Neale Hurston. He didn't know the author. Reading the back cover he learned it had been written by a black woman in 1937. The book was falling apart. Checking inside, he discovered it was a first edition and signed by the author.

His eyes slowly adjusted to this dark room. Small fans buzzed softly from bookshelves and whirred from elegant doily-draped tables. It was pleasant there.

On one of the tables was a collection of black-and-white photographs. A woman who was clearly a much younger version of this woman stood in a wedding dress beside a white man with slicked-back black hair. He looked like a gangster in the old movies Mike's parents liked to watch on *The Late Show*. There were lots of other pictures of the woman with many different people. Some were signed *to Del*; that must be her name.

But wait . . . He checked his clipboard. He had come to register a Mrs. Louisa Raymond to vote. He looked back at the autograph in *Their Eyes Were Watching God*. It said: *To my pal, Delilah Jones. Friends always! Zora Neale Hurston.*

Delilah Jones? Where had he heard the name Delilah Jones before? It wasn't déjà vu; it had been recently.

As he went to return the book, a photo fluttered from its pages. He stooped to retrieve it and froze the moment he turned it over. It showed this woman at about seventeen: radiant, bold, and lovely in a red satin dress. And at her feet sat a black panther in an emerald-studded collar — the black cat he'd seen in his mind's eye out there on the porch!

Louisa Raymond — or Delilah Jones, or whoever she was — began to stir on the couch.

"Are you Louisa Raymond?" he asked.

"Yes."

"Who is Delilah Jones?"

"I am . . . And you're Bert Brody."

"No. I'm Mike Rogers."

She nodded. "Him, too."

"I've gone back to my given first name, Louisa," she said as she poured him a glass of lemonade. They sat at her kitchen table, the sunlight through the unshaded window making the ice in the pitcher shine. Across the vinyl daisy-print tablecloth, she'd spread out more of the old photographs.

"I saw your wedding picture," he said. "Is that Mr. Raymond?"

"Lenny, yeah."

"Is your husband still alive?"

She pushed a photo of Lenny toward him. "Just before the war ended, the men who were his partners back in Chicago had him shot. By then, he was spying for the Allies and they had Axis Power sympathies. They didn't feel he'd done right by them. The war was horrible but it was good for Lenny. I think for the first time in his life it was clear to him what was right and what was wrong. The war saved his soul."

"He found his dharma," Mike murmured.

She didn't know what he meant. "I know about karma," she said. "Everybody's into it these days. The things you do come back to you, right? What's dharma?"

"It's hard to explain, and I'm not certain myself," he replied. "Do you believe in the soul?"

"Mmm," she murmured thoughtfully. "I suppose I would have to believe in it to say what I'm saying to you right now about having lived before. Do you believe in it?"

"I'm not sure."

"Of course you don't know," she said. "Only fools think they have all the answers. The universe and beyond the universe — it's so vast, so mysterious. How could anyone know everything that's going on out there?"

"I guess that's true," he agreed. "But I can't remember any lifetime other than this one."

"Do you remember being a baby, even a toddler?" she challenged him.

He shook his head. "No."

"But you know you existed."

"Yes," he admitted.

"Exactly," she said, "and besides, there are people who do remember other lives, especially under hypnosis. Back when I was a young woman in Paris, I was under the care of a Dr. LeFleur. He brought me back to several lifetimes during our hypnotic regression sessions. In the first hypnotic session I had that day I was talking about, I was a man, a soldier in the Civil War, a Yankee, and a white person."

Mike nearly sprayed his lemonade out. "You were a man?" he cried, aghast. "Is that allowed?"

This caused her to laugh uproariously. She never could get over it herself. "Apparently so! Male and *white*! Wouldn't *that* make them crazy down at the court house? I can just see it: 'Officer, I can too sit at the Whites Only lunch counter. I've already been white, black, and every shade along the way! I've been white more times than you've been born! I'm past all that now, so I'll sit where I please!'"

Mike was laughing now, too. "I would love to see that."

"Anyway," she went on, her laughter quieting, "that first session changed my life."

"How?" he asked.

"The part of that life I remembered most clearly under hypnosis was after the Civil War, opening up a pottery shop. It seems I always loved pottery, but apparently I was so jumpy around fire that I was afraid to work the kiln. So I got myself a partner. While I was hypnotized I could see her face so clearly and hear her talking to me. She was a former slave. It seems I made good on a promise to a friend by finding her after the war."

"Did it change your life because it proved reincarnation was real?" Mike asked.

"Yes, but there's more. I recognized the partner's face while I was hypnotized. She looked just like my grand-mother, Eva Jones, a former slave. My mother dumped me on her as a baby and Grandma raised me until she died when I was about four or five. I was young, but I remember. Plus, I have photos of her."

"Let me get this straight," Mike said. "You're telling me that in one life you were Eva Jones's business partner — a white man — and then you died and were reincarnated as Eva Jones's granddaughter?"

"That's it," she confirmed. "I have read a great deal on reincarnation and it's considered quite normal for people to be reborn near other people they know, often in the same family. As the white man, John Mays, I must have felt quite fondly toward Eva, so I came back as her granddaughter in order to continue to be near her. It makes perfect sense if you think about it."

"It does make sense when you put it that way," Mike admitted.

"And then, as a young woman, I met you — when you were Bert Brody — and you told me how your grandfather had been the founder of Mays' Dishware and he had been afraid of fire and had a partner and such. Did some research and discovered that the company had originally, from 1870 to 1910, been called Mays and Jones Pottery — John Mays and Eva Jones."

"Your grandmother was a partner in Mays' Dishware?" Mike asked.

"You got it. John Mays died in 1910 and Eva Jones sold her half of the business to his nephew — who was his heir — because she was getting too old to work. She was nearly eighty when she died, leaving no will. No one knew she had any heirs. But, apparently I had a big inheritance coming. By then the government had taken most of her unclaimed money. When I came forward as her granddaughter I was able to claim this house and, hidden in a closet, I found a pile of Mays Dishware stock that was worth a bundle of money."

Mike put his hands on his head and squeezed.

"Is it too confusing?" Louisa asked.

"So you inherited stock money from the company that you yourself had helped found in an earlier incarnation?"

She shook her head at the sheer incredibility of the story. "Yes! Isn't that wild? It killed my singing career, unfortunately. Since I no longer *needed* to work — I didn't! It's been a fun life, though — at least once World War Two ended — I've been traveling and whooping it up."

"How did you end up back here?"

"This was Grandma's house. I couldn't sell it, and as I got older, it seemed a good place to settle down."

"Do you have any regrets?" Mike asked her.

"One. I recorded an album of songs. It's not available anymore. I'd like to hear it again."

"You said I was Bert Brody."

"I believe you are, yes."

"Why do you think so?"

"I feel it. I had a few hypnotic sessions that went into the future, like premonitions. I may have seen you then."

"Who was he?"

"A songwriter I knew. The songs on the album are written by him."

"I write songs now."

"Well, there you go."

Mike jumped up, knocking the ice from his glass. "That's where I heard the name Delilah Jones before!" he cried. "I listened to your record last night!"

"Where?"

"It was sitting on an old record player. I thought it was so great that I wanted to tape it for myself. It's in the trunk of my car. I'll be right back!"

Mike's head was spinning as he returned to the sweltering, sun-drenched outside world. Inside, in Louisa's darkened, cool house, it was easy to believe her. Out here in the hard light of reality he began to doubt. Her story was so fantastic.

He was this Bert Brody?

She had inherited money from her own past-life self?

He hurried down the steps to his car, his mind working out the various connections. Was everyone's past so entangled, so connected to a previous lifetime?

He stopped and shook his head. She was just putting him on — having some fun with the naïve, dumb white college kid.

That was it.

It had to be.

She'd probably loaned this record to a friend and knew it was on the turntable at the place they were staying.

Ha-ha! Very funny. Have a big laugh at the do-gooder dope from up North.

He was astounded at his own stupidity.

The woman had really had him going, though. What an *idiot* he was! What a good actress she was.

His face grew hot from within and he knew he was blushing. Mortified and embarrassed, he got into his car and sped away.

Louisa stood at her window and watched Mike drive off. She'd scared him. It wasn't his fault. It had taken her more than twenty years to come to terms with the revelations she'd come upon under hypnosis with Dr. LeFleur.

"Humph." A laugh burbled up inside her. "Imagine, me — a nun. If that doesn't beat everything." At first that lifetime had been the hardest for her to believe, but she'd finally come to understand it. Her devotion as a nun to Mary the Virgin Mother of Jesus was totally fitting when she lined it up with the other lives she'd uncovered.

She took a holy card showing a Black Madonna and child from her dress pocket. The image was known as Our Lady of Czestochowa from Poland, and it dated from the thirteenth or fourteenth century. Turning it over in her hand, she gazed at the dark-skinned figures. She loved this picture and sometimes wondered if she had loved it when she was Mother Abbess Maria Regina. To her it was Mary and all the other goddesses she had ever revered rolled into one. At any rate, she found it comforting and liked to look at it often.

Someone rapped at the front door. Not waiting for an answer, a woman stuck her head in the door. "Louisa?"

"Right here, Birdy. Come in."

The slim young woman in a nurse's uniform stepped into the room. She was of obviously mixed race with a wide spray of freckles across her dark olive skin. Her tight red curls were bundled neatly to the back of her head, though stray strands coiled prettily around her cheeks and greenish, amber-flecked eyes. She wore a yellow cardigan over her uniform. "How are you doing today, Miss Louisa?" she asked.

"Not bad," Louisa replied. "I just had a visit from one of those young voter registration people."

"I give them credit," Birdy said, putting down her purse. "The whites down here are giving them a terrible time. It's like the Civil War is still being fought. There's a bunch of them living down the road here in Arthur Adams's grandma's old place, the one that was empty for so long."

"I know the place."

"How's the ankle today?"

"It hurts."

"Sit down, let's unwrap that Ace bandage and have a look at it."

Birdy was a practical nurse working in the Colored Only clinic. One day when Louisa was there consulting with the doctor about her cancer, she'd struck up a conversation with Birdy while waiting. When Birdy asked why Louisa used a cane, she'd told her how her right ankle had never been right. Birdy had said, "I pass your house on my way home. I should stop by and check up on you to make sure you haven't fallen. Now, with your other problems, you could be too weak to get up."

"You don't have to do that," Louisa had replied.

"I'd like to," Birdy had insisted. "It would give me some experience. If I can ever save the money, I'd like to go to nursing school for my RN degree and become a full nurse. Maybe I could go to Howard University."

So now Birdy came to check on Louisa twice a week.

Louisa sat on one of her fat upholstered chairs and hoisted her leg onto the ottoman. "That looks a little swollen," Birdy commented as she unwrapped the bandage. "Have you been on it a lot today?"

"No, but I had a fall earlier."

"A fall?"

"I fainted."

"The heat?" Birdy asked.

Louisa didn't have the strength to go into the whole story. "Probably."

Birdy stood. "I'm going to run you a bath and put Epsom salts into it. It will do you good to soak your ankle, and a cool bath in this weather couldn't hurt you, either. Did you hit your head when you fell?"

"I don't think so. It doesn't hurt."

Birdy rewrapped Louisa's ankle and helped her up from the chair, giving her the cane.

"Birdy," Louisa asked, "have you ever heard of dharma?"

"Nope."

"Heard of karma?"

"Like, what goes around comes around?"

"Yes. How long do you think it takes for what goes around to come back around?"

Birdy laughed as she walked with Louisa to the stairs. "I'm sure I have no idea."

"The young man who was just here was telling me about dharma. It means doing one's spiritual duty, the thing you were put in this life to do."

"*This* life?" Birdy questioned. "What other life is there?"

"Okay, say there's none other. It's what you were put in this one life to do," Louisa said. Birdy was a practical young woman and a strict Baptist. The idea of other lives would no doubt be promptly rejected. "Do you feel you are doing what you were meant to do in this life?"

"That's a big question, Miss Louisa," Birdy answered with a smile. "All I know is that right now I am helping you up these stairs and attending to that ankle."

That night, back with the other volunteers, Mike felt exhausted. He'd covered fifty homes after leaving Louisa's place and had signed up only ten voters. The other volunteers had had similar experiences.

"I thought your brother was going to punch the cop who pulled us over," said one of the girls who had gone out with Ray. "That cop was just plain hassling us, demanding the car registration and my license, wanting to know everything about us. It was harassment."

"I wanted to deck the guy," Ray confirmed. "I couldn't believe it."

"Now do you think I'm paranoid?" the handbook girl asked.

"I guess I owe you an apology," Ray conceded.

"Apology accepted," she said.

Wow, cool, Mike thought, impressed. *Ray's apologizing to someone — will wonders never cease?* Of course, he was apologizing to a girl, probably trying to score points with her. Still . . . Mike wouldn't have expected it of Ray.

"It's important to keep your cool with the local law," Dave counseled. "They're looking for any reason to arrest you — and you do *not* want to get locked up."

Throughout supper, Mike kept up social conversation, but his mind wasn't really on it. Finally he got the chance he'd been dying for all day. After the plates were cleaned and the next day's activities discussed, he was free to place the record of Delilah Jones singing the songs of Bert Brody back on the record player.

He couldn't stop thinking about her — and it wasn't only because of the strangeness of what she'd told him. It was the woman herself. She was much too old for him, but he found her lovely in a way he could never imagine himself feeling about a woman of her age. The idea of it put him off, but the actuality of her drew him in. She'd captivated him.

Delilah Jones's voice drifted up from the record. Funny that she'd been afraid of fire, because her voice reminded him of smoke. He closed his eyes as it billowed around him. Could he really have written these songs? They were different from the songs he wrote now — in many ways better.

Ray strolled out onto the porch, letting the screen door slam behind him. "What are you listening to?"

"'Delilah Jones Sings the Songs of Bert Brody,'" he replied. "I found it on the record player."

Ray blinked twice, as though he was struggling to understand what Mike was telling him. He perched on the porch railing and looked out over the fields.

"It's an old record from the thirties," Mike explained.

"Del Jones has some pipes," Ray commented.

Mike turned to him sharply. "Why did you call her Del?"

Ray tore his gaze from the field and, looking at Mike, shrugged. "I don't know. Why are you so jumpy about it?"

"Something really bizarre happened to me today," he began.

"Stranger than almost clobbering a cop?"

"Yeah. Stranger than that." As the record played, Mike

began to tell his brother about meeting Louisa — Delilah Jones.

"You met *this* woman, the one who's singing now?" Ray asked.

"I was in her house. She had stuff around with the name Delilah Jones on it. She said I was Bert Brody."

"What?"

"She said she knew me in another life."

"That's nuts," Ray remarked, returning to looking out over the fields. "What a kook. Maybe she's a witch. Did she look like a wrinkled old hag?"

"No . . . she was beautiful."

"I'll bet," Ray scoffed.

Mike continued to tell him what Delilah had said. "What if it *is* true?" Mike wondered out loud when he was finished. "If she knew Bert Brody and I'm him, maybe she and I have unfinished business. Her husband might have been reborn, too. Why not?"

"Don't be a sap," Ray said.

There was a catch in his voice that got Mike's attention.

"Is something the matter?" Mike asked.

Ray continued to stare out over the fields without answering, so Mike stood and went beside him. "You okay?"

Ray's eyes were wet and his nose had reddened as though he wanted to cry but was fighting it. Mike had never seen Ray even close to tears. "What is it?"

He sniffed hard and pressed his arm into his eyes before turning to Mike. "It's this idiotic record. It's annoying me." He slid off the railing and headed for the door. "Turn it off, will you? It's aggravating."

Mystified, Mike watched him go in. He shut the record off and took it from the turntable. With it under his arm, he got into his car and drove through the brightly lit night to Louisa's house.

The house was dark but the porch was lit from above. Louisa sat on her front porch step, as though waiting for him.

"Here's that record." He spoke matter-of-factly, as if he had gone to his car and come directly back.

Louisa smiled at him. "What took you so long?"

"I got scared," he admitted.

"I don't blame you."

He sat beside her on the step, handing her the record. "Yeah, well . . . I'm back now."

She rested her hand on his. "I'm glad," she said.

The next weeks were filled with highs and lows for Ray. The young woman he went out recruiting with was named Linda. He'd attached himself to her, thinking she was the best-looking girl there. In other words, his perfect partner. Along the way, going door to door with her, he also discovered that she had a way with people and was smart and well-informed. *And* he discovered that she had a boyfriend back home. But by then it was okay with him. He'd come to think of her more as a partner and a pal.

Besides, he'd met a young woman in town, a nurse named Birdy. He'd gone into the hospital for help with a badly scraped shoulder. He'd fallen on it when a protective dog chased him from the front porch of one of the run-down homes he and Linda were approaching.

The nurse at the admitting desk had sized him up immediately from his northern accent. "You're one of those volunteers?" she'd asked. When he admitted it, she'd said, "Try the Colored Only Clinic. They're your friends. We're not."

"Fine. I will," he'd told her.

Linda had driven him to a run-down building at the edge of town. "It's against the law for us to treat you in here," the nurse there told him. "But I'll send somebody out to you. Wait outside."

Birdy came out and attended to his cuts, applying iodine that stung. They talked like they'd known each other all their lives. "How long is your shift?" he asked.

"I work until four."

Ray dropped Linda back at the headquarters house and made it back to the clinic by four. "Want a ride home?" he offered as Birdy walked out of the clinic.

"I can't be seen with you," she told him. "It's too dangerous. People don't like to see couples of mixed races."

"You don't look like a Negro," he noted.

"I'm half, and everyone around here knows it. Ma met my white father up North, but he ran out on her, so she came back home here with me."

"How can I see you then?" he asked.

She thought about this, looking him up and down. "My house is way out of town. I live there with my mother and little brothers. If anyone asks — and I hope they don't — you could say you're trying to convince us to vote. We don't want to have anything to do with it, but you're not giving up."

She scrawled directions on a medical pad and then hurried away. "We eat at seven. You're welcome if you like," she said over her shoulder as she departed.

Ray arrived that night at her simple, neat house with a box of chocolates and a bouquet of flowers he'd bought in town. "I'm thanking your daughter for fixing my shoulder for me," he told Birdy's mother to deflect any suspicions about his possible ulterior motives.

Her mother just sniffed suspiciously, nodding as though to say, *You're not fooling me, young man.*

Her two smaller brothers were playing a game that involved hurling a straight branch over a line they'd drawn in the dirt. "All right!" Ray cheered. "A javelin toss! Let me at it!"

He gave the boys pointers that greatly increased their

success. "I threw the javelin in college," he explained as he went to fetch a stick that had gotten off course.

"Look out," he heard Birdy's mother warn her while they watched the game from the bench outside. "You're asking for trouble."

Louisa should have been feeling worse than she felt. At her last trip to the doctor, he'd told her he believed that she didn't have much time left. "It could be months. It could be weeks," he'd reported.

She'd nodded. "Okay." This wasn't really news. Her body had been telling her for some time that things were worsening.

On the way out of the clinic, she ran into Birdy. "How's it going, sweetie?" she asked.

Birdy looked especially upbeat. "Just great," she replied.

"Birdy has a new boyfriend," another of the nurses blurted.

"Hush up," Birdy hissed at her. "It's a secret."

"It is," the other nurse told Louisa. "She won't let any of us meet him. Rumor is that he's a volunteer."

"I said hush," Birdy said. "He's not."

"I wouldn't mind one of those nice college-educated black men to whisk me away from here and take me up North," the nurse said. "That Julian Bond is quite handsome."

"The young man with the NAACP?" Louisa asked.

"Yes, him," the nurse said. "Are you dating Julian Bond, Birdy?"

"Be quiet!" Birdy pretended to be angry but her smile gave her away.

Louisa was happy for Birdy. Feelings of romance — both memories and new emotions — were very much with her these days. "Listen, Birdy, I won't need you to come by this week," she said. "I have a guest visiting."

"Okay, if you're sure you'll be all right."

"Absolutely. Thanks."

Mike had been coming by every night for the last two weeks. She made him leave if Birdy was coming by, so as not to cause any talk. Not that Birdy would gossip, but Louisa didn't want to take the chance that she'd mention something at home and her mother would spread it.

It would be shocking enough that she was keeping company with a white man — the fact that he was nearly thirty years younger than she was would be an outrage. No one would believe that they never touched each other, though it was the truth. Their age difference made them each too shy of it. But they loved each other, nonetheless.

When she got back to her house, Mike's car was already parked outside. He came out from inside the house and helped her up the walk. "How did it go?" he asked, taking her elbow.

"The ankle is fine," she said. She hadn't mentioned the cancer. He thought her bad ankle was her only problem.

"I made us some chicken fricassee for supper," he told her. "And a woman I signed up to vote gave me a tub of her homemade ice cream."

"It sounds divine."

The days rolled on like this. Louisa felt happier than she had ever felt. To her, the heartbreaking loss of her old love had been mended, restored to her. Her heart felt whole again.

Mike talked about all the feelings and thoughts that he swore he had never revealed to another person.

"Sometimes I don't know why I'm here doing this," he admitted to her. "It seems so hopeless."

"You've always hated slavery," she said. "I believe you've been dealing with slavery in one form or another for many lives."

"You do?" he asked. "Why do you think so?"

She wasn't exactly sure how she knew it, yet she knew. "I feel it," she said. "This is what you must do to be right with your past."

"I don't have too much past at this point."

"You have more than you think," she told him. "Get me one of those registration forms. I think I will register to vote, after all."

Then one day while he was playing guitar for her in the

living room and singing her one of the songs he'd written, a car came up the road and made a quick and abrupt stop.

Ducking from under his guitar strap, Mike stepped to the window and pushed the lace curtains aside.

Louisa was already locking the doors and windows.

"It's okay," he told her. "It's Dave from our group."

Louisa followed Mike out onto the porch. "Come quick," Dave said breathlessly. "Ray's been arrested. He's been seeing a local black woman and they tried to sit in the Whites Only section of the movie theater."

"Ray?" Mike questioned.

"Yeah," Dave said. "We can't let either of them stay in jail overnight. I don't want to think about what could happen. They've set a six-thousand-dollar bail on each one of them."

"Twelve thousand!" Mike cried. "I can call home, but I don't think my parents have that kind of money."

"We've started a collection, but we don't have nearly enough," Dave told him.

"Just a minute," Louisa said to Dave. "Let me talk to Mike inside." Taking Mike's wrist, she went back into the house. "Listen to me," she said. "I have given away just about all that's left of my inheritance for reasons which I can tell you later. But I do have one thing of value left which I kept for sentimental reasons."

She opened the lower door of a china cabinet to reveal a safe. With deft fingers she opened the combination and pulled out a shiny wooden box. Inside was a thick collar studded with eight glistening emeralds. "You take this downtown to O'Hara's Jewelry Store. Mr. O'Hara knows what it's worth. I had it appraised there. He will want to buy it from you right away. He's told me so many times."

She wrote the address of the store on a piece of paper. "I'll call to tell him you're coming so he doesn't think you stole it," she said, handing him the paper.

"I can't take this," he objected.

"It is my dharma to give it to you," she said. "Go."

Mike raced into the police building behind Dave. A crowd of the volunteers poured in behind him.

"We have the bail money for Raymond Rogers and Bernadette Towers," Dave shouted at the desk sergeant. "We demand that they be released immediately. If either of them has been harmed we will bring a lawsuit that will bankrupt this county!"

"Hold your horses. They're okay," the sergeant muttered, eyeing them all with disgust. "Come here and fill out the paperwork. You're going to have to send somebody else in to get Miss Towers. You have to send a colored to go in through the colored door."

Dave turned to Mike. "Ernie Long is signing up voters down at the school auditorium," he told him. "Tell him to come down here to get Miss Towers."

"Okay," Mike agreed. He counted out the money he'd

gotten from Mr. O'Hara. Ernie Long was a good choice. He was seemingly fearless. He could negotiate any problem that might arise.

Mike hurried out of the police station. The sun blazed overhead, blinding him. His arm was raised to shield his eyes as he stepped off the curb.

He never saw the speeding car that rounded the corner and tossed him into the air.

Then

I am flying.

My body drops to the ground . . . but I keep going, light as a feather.

I don't bother to watch the commotion below. I need to get back to Louisa.

When I soar over her house, she is sitting on the roof. She reaches her arms up to me. She is young again like when I first saw her sing at The Panther: Isis, the nicest on the Nile.

I remember now! I remember! Everything she told me is true!

Below, on the porch, her older self sleeps in her rocking chair. Her face is content.

I sit beside her spirit on the peak of the roof.

My arms are around her. We kiss — such a deep, long kiss.

How could it be that I didn't recognize my heart's true love the minute I saw her? What took me so long?

Down on the porch, someone coughs.

Sliding to the edge of the roof, I bend forward to see who it is.

Older Louisa has awakened, not dead as I had believed! She rubs her eyes and slowly pulls herself from her rocker.

Frantically, I check the roof.

My young Louisa is no longer there!

I slide down to the ground beside her as she hobbles toward the road. "Louisa!" I cry. "What happened?"

I know what happened.

Her body rallied and called her spirit back.

I should be glad but I'm not. For a moment I had my love and now I don't. I'm disappointed and angry.

"I'm here," I say desperately. She turns toward my voice, almost hearing it, though not quite sure what is calling her. Is it the boll weevils rustling the grass, the sweltering buzz of heat rising off the road?

Louisa stands in the dusty road, leaning on her cane, waiting for me to drive back, to return to her. A hot breeze flattens her skirt against her legs. She knows something is wrong. It's on her face.

Out in the middle of the cotton field stands an angel.

I know I must go. To remain as a ghost would be to witness more sorrow, bear more loneliness than I can stand.

"Good-bye, my Louisa. You have shown me how it is. I know now that you have been right about the past lives, about everything. Forgive me for thinking you were a little crazy. It didn't matter to me, anyway, if you were. I loved you more this time than ever before. You are my dharma, my dear one."

The angel is beside me. Like a Great Bird he rises, taking me with him.

New York, the present

Samantha Tyler shut her eyes and let the music on her iPod flood her head. Outside the moving school bus, the buildings slowly increased in height as they approached Manhattan for their senior geology class outing to the American Museum of Natural History.

She wished she could have skipped school this Friday. Her audition for Juilliard's college music division was tomorrow. It would have been good if she could have practiced singing her tryout songs or even rested. But this trip was required by her science teacher, so there was no way out of it.

A tap on her shoulder made her jump.

"You were singing along with the iPod again," her friend Zoë said from the seat beside her. "Loud." Zoë zipped up her yellow Abercrombie hoodie and fluffed her long red curls. "I have to talk to you. It's serious."

"What?"

Zoë lowered her voice. "You told me last night that you were thinking of breaking up with Chris, right?"

"Right." Samantha ducked lower in the seat so no one would see they were talking. "Don't tell anyone. I don't want Chris to find out before I talk to him. That would be nasty."

"I won't," Zoë assured her. "Are you sure you want to do it? He *is* captain of the football team, after all. I mean, he's hot."

"He's a great guy, too. But . . . I don't know. He just doesn't get me," Samantha said. It was a hard-to-explain difference that she couldn't figure out. Chris was nice but somehow they just didn't connect.

"Maybe you don't get him," Zoë suggested.

"It could be," Samantha admitted.

"Have you definitely made up your mind to break up with him?"

"No. Why?"

Zoë scowled. "Oh. I was just thinking that if you had decided that you wanted to break up with him, you could do it today while we're at the museum. Then, if he didn't take it well, you could give him the slip for the rest of the day and it wouldn't be as awkward as if you broke up with him on a regular school day."

"True," Samantha agreed. "Why is this so important to you?"

"You're my friend," Zoë replied.

Samantha eyed her suspiciously. Zoë wanted to go out with Chris. Samantha had suspected it for a while and now she was sure. She couldn't say she wouldn't mind. It would be weird to have her friend go out with her ex-boyfriend. But it wouldn't break her heart, either. "I'll let you know what I decide," she told Zoë.

"I think you really like that new guy, Jake Suarez, more," Zoë suggested.

"Do you mean the one who won the archery tournament last Saturday?" Samantha asked.

Zoë poked her. "You are so full of it. You know exactly who I mean. I saw you watching him in the cafeteria the other day."

"I don't know him," Samantha said. "He's not in any of my classes. But he seems nice and he's cute."

"I knew you liked him," Zoë said.

Samantha swiveled in her seat and looked at Chris sitting at the back of the bus with his football buddies. He noticed her and waved.

She returned the wave and intentionally caught a glimpse of Jake as she turned back around. He was plugged into an MP3 player and reading at the same time: a beat-up paperback called *Siddhartha.*

Zoë was more right than she knew. Jake was new to the school and from the first instant Samantha saw him he'd gotten to her. She knew exactly when it was. He'd been out on the archery field all alone, probably practicing for the tournament in which he eventually took first place.

She had stopped her trek across the field, riveted by the picture he made: glistening dark curls, straight strong back, his arms pulled back, and his total focus on the target in front of him.

He hit the bull's-eye in the center of the target.

In that moment she was completely gone; he was all she could think about from then on. Her relationship with Chris went flat almost the next day. It wasn't fair to him, she knew. But her attraction to Jake was fiercely undeniable. It didn't feel like she had any choice in the matter.

"You're right," she told Zoë. "I'm going to break up with Chris."

"Would you hate me if I . . . you know," Zoë asked, staring down at her hands folded uneasily in her lap.

"You like him, don't you?"

Zoë nodded.

"It would be okay with me," Samantha said.

Looking up at Samantha, Zoë smiled. "You're sure?"

"It's no big deal. Chris and I have only been going out for a month. I think you and Chris are more suited for each other, anyway."

They went through the Midtown Tunnel into Manhattan and drove uptown and through Central Park until they came to the museum. The majestic building with its columns and wide steps struck Samantha as oddly familiar, but she couldn't think of why that might be.

They went into the main entry with its colossal, towering dinosaur skeletons and paid the entry fee, which included access to the planetarium, all halls and special shows, and the IMAX movie playing that day: *Comets — Crashes and Collisions.*

Samantha asked Chris if they could talk even before

they went into the main part of the museum. "I don't know how to say this," she began.

"You want to break up," he said.

"You knew?"

"It wasn't hard to tell when you didn't even want to sit with me on the bus," he explained.

"Sorry," she said, wrinkling her forehead. "You're great but I just think we're real . . . you know . . . different."

"Yeah, we are," he agreed. "Okay. See ya."

"See ya." Samantha watched as he ran after a group of his friends, thumping one of them on the back in greeting. She breathed a sigh of relief. That had been easier than she'd expected.

Looking around the hall, she realized none of her classmates or teachers were still there. Not wanting to be on her own the whole day, she hurried into the museum.

The place was enormous! Where had all the others gone so fast? She grabbed a floor plan and a schedule of museum events from the stack on a stand. There were certain places they were required by their teachers to go that day. The kids had probably all raced to those spots first to get them out of the way.

She hurried through the shadowy, high-ceilinged halls lined with glassed-in life-size dioramas of different taxidermied animals posed as though they were in their natural habitats. The murals in the background made the scenes appear amazingly lifelike.

Up ahead, she spied Jake Suarez standing alone, peering into one of the cases.

How perfect was this? When would she ever get another chance to talk to him alone this way, under such a totally plausible pretext?

With her heart beating like accelerated time, she approached him.

"Thank God I found somebody from our school," she said, coming up alongside him. "I'm Samantha. You're new in school, aren't you?"

He turned to her and his hazel eyes were unfocused, as though she'd disturbed thoughts that had taken him very far away. "Yeah, I'm Jake. Hi."

"Do you know where everyone went to?" she asked. "It's like they disappeared."

"I think they all rushed up to the Hall of Gems to see that emerald show we have to report on. I was on my way, too, but I stopped to look at this display."

Inside the glass, a stuffed bison grazed tranquilly. The rest of the herd had been painted into the mural behind the bull. "What a beautiful animal," he remarked.

"A lot of people would think he was ugly," Samantha pointed out. "But I see what you mean."

"They have drawings of them on cave walls that are still around today."

"So are we," she mentioned.

He looked at her sharply, as though startled by her words.

"People, I mean," she clarified. "We're still around, too. What did you think I meant?"

"I don't know . . . nothing. I guess . . . I was just confused for a second. Want to go to that gem thing?"

"We might as well," she said, doing her best not to reveal how excited she was to be walking down the hall beside him. This was fate! It had to be! What were the chances of running into him alone like this? Did he know how much she liked him? Had he noticed her watching him every time he went by?

Then she was struck with a new, exciting thought: Had he lagged behind intentionally, noticing that she was behind him? Was he really there waiting for her?

She gazed at him from the corner of her eye. Was that what had happened? Did he feel the same attraction — the same *connection* — that she did? Oh, how she hoped so.

As they headed toward the Hall of Gems they talked about their college applications. He'd been accepted to the Pace University Theater Department. "I can't wait to take their playwriting and screenwriting courses," he said.

"Have you written any plays?" she asked.

"I got a scholarship based on this screenplay I wrote that was set during the Salem Witch Trials."

"What happened in it?" she asked as they turned the corner.

"It's about this sailor who meets a girl he's crazy about and he gives her these earrings as a sign of his love. But her father doesn't approve of him and one night when he's trying to see the girl, the father chases him with a gun."

"Pretty dramatic," she commented.

He laughed. "I know. I have this crazy imagination. Wait. It gets wilder. The father ships the daughter off to America to marry this creep lawyer and he finds the earrings that the girl has stashed away. He gets so consumed with jealousy that he turns the girl over as a witch and she's burned at the stake."

"Oh, that must be a horrible, horrible way to die," Samantha said as a shiver ran through her. She could see it somehow, as though she was looking out through the woman's eyes; she saw faces jeering at her. She smelled the acrid burning of the straw as it began to ignite.

The hallway seemed to spin and Samantha lost her footing. She gripped Jake's arm to steady herself.

"Are you okay?" he asked, guiding her toward a bench.

"I'm sorry, I got dizzy all of a sudden. I just need to sit a minute. Go on with your story."

"Okay," he agreed. "Are you sure you're all right?"

"I will be. Go on."

"Anyway, she doesn't know that the sailor has come looking for her. He gets there too late to save her, but sees the earrings there in the ashes of the fire and knows she was wearing them at the stake as a sign of her love for him. He gets the earrings out of the fire and throws them into the Atlantic Ocean."

"He came back for her and she didn't know it?" Samantha asked. She wanted to cry. Why was this story affecting her so strongly? "That's the saddest story," she said.

"I know," he agreed. "The saddest part to me is that she died not knowing he had come looking for her. The sailor feels so horrible, like if he'd only gotten there sooner he might have saved her. He blames himself for the rest of his life."

"He shouldn't have," she said. "He tried his best."

"He should never have let her go in the first place. He was an idiot," Jake said passionately. "He deserved to be miserable for the rest of his life."

"You're too hard on him."

"He's my character. I can be hard on him." He sat beside her, seemingly lost in thought. Then he turned to her. "Feeling any better?"

"Uh-huh," she said, standing. "It's a great story."

"It got me a scholarship, anyhow."

"How'd you think of it?"

"I don't know. Stories are always popping into my head."

As they walked through the museum, she told him about her upcoming audition. "I wasn't sure whether to apply to their vocal department or their dance department," she confessed. "I can probably study it all under Performing Arts."

"I saw you in the school play," he told her. "You were amazing. I saw you at the gymnastic performance on the balance beam, too. Man, you rocked it. First place!"

"Thanks. Why were you there?"

"My brother, Ato, was on the rings."

"Oh, yeah, he was good," she recalled.

"You're so surefooted," he commented.

"Thank you. It's a good thing I wore orthopedic shoes as a kid. I was born with a foot that was turned in, but the orthopedist corrected it and it's fine now."

"You'd never know," he said.

They had arrived at the Hall of Gems. The large poster in front of the room announced the special show the museum had mounted. It read: FAMOUS EMERALDS THROUGH THE AGES. Just as they'd thought, lots of their classmates were inside taking notes on the many displays.

They took out their notebooks as they moved together past the displays. The room was heavily staffed with security guards who kept their eyes on the priceless emeralds locked in glass cases. One of the largest was from Peru. "I can see why they worshipped this thing," Samantha said as she read the plaque beside it. "It's so amazing."

The green riches were nearly overwhelming, each emerald larger and more spectacular than the last.

Her eyes locked on an item in its own case. "Look at this emerald-studded collar," she said, peering into the case.

"That's crazy," he agreed, stooping to examine it more closely. "I can just picture it on some kind of big cat."

"You must be psychic," she commented, coming upon a picture on the placard beside it. The black-and-white photo showed a beautiful dark-skinned woman in a satiny halter dress. She was about seventeen. And at her feet sat a black panther in an emerald-studded collar.

"Let me see that?" Jake said, standing beside her. "Delilah Jones," he read. He looked up sharply at Samantha. "You look just like her."

Samantha peered at the photo. "I don't think there's any resemblance at all," she disagreed.

"It's in the eyes," he insisted. "You have the same eyes."

They both studied the photo. Maybe he was right. There was something in Delilah Jones's eyes that spoke to her deeply, as if she were looking directly into her innermost self.

"What are you humming?" he asked her.

"Was I humming?" she asked, embarrassed. "I didn't even realize it."

"Yes, you were humming. I know the song but I can't think of its name. It sounded like an old song."

She shook her head, bewildered. "Sorry. I didn't know I was doing it. It's gone from my head now."

"Too bad. It was pretty," he said, gazing at her intently.

"Why are you looking at me like that?" she asked.

He smiled apologetically. "Sorry. Every time I look at you I feel like I'm trying to remember something that I can't get a hold of."

"Me, too," she said.

"Really?"

"Really." When she looked at him she felt it, too. It was something she felt was just out of reach, like trying to recall someone's name that she once knew but could no longer quite call to mind.

"How freaky," he remarked, still studying her.

"It is," she agreed.

They continued walking through the hall. There were emerald rings and necklaces salvaged from the wrecks of Spanish galleons. An Eye of Horus pendant with an emerald set in the center had survived from ancient Egypt. The information card said it was among the treasures Alexander the Great sent back to Athens after he conquered Egypt in 332 B.C.E. A headdress called the Crown of Andes was set with 453 emeralds. It was named for Atahualpa, one of the last emperors of the Incas, who was taken captive by Pizarro in 1532.

"There's so much death and fighting attached to these emeralds," Samantha observed.

"I know," Jake agreed.

Under a banner that read FABULOUS FAKES were gems that were often mistaken for emeralds. There was a carving of Buddha made from a tall emerald, labeled the Emerald Buddha. "It's really green jasper," Jake told her, reading the information card beside it.

A clump of green crystal was labeled EMERALD CRYSTALS IN CALCITE MATRIX WITH PYRITE FORMATIONS. "Read this card," Jake told her.

Leaning close, Samantha read. The crystals had been found clenched in the fingers of a male Neanderthal skeleton that had been washed ashore by the rushing water into which he had apparently fallen from a cliff above. His bones were entangled with those of another skeleton believed to be those of a Cro-Magnon female, the prehistoric figure most resembling people today. The archeologists who uncovered them suspected that these two had died struggling for the rock.

"Write a play about that," Samantha suggested to Jake. "That's about as tragic as it gets. They died fighting for a rock."

"I know. Stupid, huh?"

They came to a display marked EVENING PERIDOT, BELIEVED TO BE ORIGINALLY FROM THE RED SEA ISLAND OF ST. JOHN'S. FOUND WASHED ASHORE ON THE ATLANTIC COAST. It was a single, lovely green drop earring.

They stood together, silent, staring down at it. It was strange: Samantha felt a lump forming in her throat and came near to crying.

Jake noticed. "Are you okay?" he asked.

Was there a catch in his voice as well?

Not wanting to speak for fear of crying, she nodded. After a moment, she felt able to talk. "Maybe it's just that ... it's how I pictured the earring in your story."

"Me, too," he agreed quietly. "It's not even a real emerald."

"Who cares," said Samantha. "It's beautiful."

"It is," he agreed. "And they found it here in the Atlantic, even though it comes from the Caribbean."

"Like in your story," Samantha said.

"Like in my story. Weird."

"In your play, he came back for her, right?" she checked.

"Uh-huh. But he was too late."

They continued to gaze at the earring. She wanted to take hold of his hand, suddenly feeling strangely close to him, but fought the urge. She didn't know him well enough for that.

"Hey," he said, looking up after a while, "where did everybody go?"

Samantha checked the schedule of events. "The IMAX comet movie starts in two minutes," she told him. "Want to try to make it?"

"Yeah."

Following the museum map, they made their way to the IMAX theater, showed their tickets, and hurried into the already-darkened theater.

"Can you see any empty seats?" she whispered to him.

"No."

After a moment though, she spied a single empty seat right on the end. She went for it at the same moment Jake tried to sit in it. They bounced off each other there in the dark, their heads clacking together painfully.

"Ow!" she cried.

"Shh!" came a chorus of voices.

"Are you all right?" he whispered. She could tell he was rubbing his head also.

"I'll live," she said.

"Want to share the seat?" he offered.

"Yeah."

Carefully, they both perched on the corners of the seat, squeezed against each other. She found being so close to him exciting and oddly easy all at the same time.

On the enormous screen, the planet Earth rose before them from the vantage point of a passing comet. It hovered in the darkness in its entire blue and green splendor — a green, turning orb more shining and gorgeous than any emerald.

This time, she didn't hesitate. She took hold of his hand.

He turned to her there in the dark. She waited, not daring to breathe. What would he do?

He squeezed her hand. "Is it just me?" he whispered. "Have I known you forever?"

"I'm so glad you feel it, too," she whispered in reply, relieved to hear him say what she felt. "This thing between us . . . is it real?"

"It's real," he assured her. "Don't ask me how I know, but it is. We wouldn't both be feeling it if it wasn't."

Samantha knew that this was the beginning of the rest of her life. Her life would be with him from now on. They would never be apart again.

It didn't matter how or why she knew it. She knew.

This was it.

They'd made it.

Together they gazed at the screen in front of them as if out into the universe: The Earth and the vast, fathomless universe — the mysterious green jewel spinning in the darkness — all there for them to share, as it had been from the start.